SUMMER RAY

This Fair and Blighted Land

Written By: Juliana Love

1

Website: authorjulianalove.com
Website: thememoirsofsummerray.com
Facebook: The Memoirs of Summer Ray

LOVE Studios L.L.C.
Round Top Publishers
P.O. Box 4166
Gettysburg, PA 17325

Twitter & Instagram @JLuv1023

THEY MAY HAVE DIED AS ENEMIES...

BUT WERE RESURRECTED

AS BROTHERS!

DEDICATION

My beloved children
Nicole, Susan, Chris & Taylor
You all will forever remain my pride and joy!

My son and daughter in law
Emily & Kevin
I thank God we are so blessed to have you in our
family.

Hendrix Skye, Azariah Christopher, Cillian Christopher
Wow! There are no words to describe how much your
Gammie loves you!

The DeTello Family
Jessica without you this series would not have been
possible!

My God
You are forever "My Everything!"

IN LOVING MEMORY OF

Mrs. Nancy Pritchett

aka

The Matron Duvall

I can still hear your sweet voice and see your beautiful face. You are missed more than you could possibly know.

I will also remember our time together, though very short, it will stay with me throughout a lifetime.

Our movie Matron Duvall – will be forever yours as no one could ever take your place.

Juliana

ACKNOWLEDGEMENT

Carole Lee Dean

From the Heart Productions

Thank you for believing in me and in the story of Summer Ray. I KNOW God sent me to you. I look forward to working with you on our upcoming features of this story. You're one of the miracles I prayed for. Thank You God for answering!

FROM THE SUMMER RAY

BOOK SERIES

TO

THE SUMMER RAY FILM SAGA

TABLE OF CONTENTS

MISSION STATEMENT

Jesus did not come to call those who are well. He came to seek the lost, the hurting and the sick. Our mission at Love Studios L.L.C., (the umbrella over Round Top Publishers, Everwood Entites, and J & J Photography) is to bring quality stories and films to reach those who desperately need:

- To be encouraged by the Word of God
- To be set free from demonic oppression
- To know the truth, so that the truth can set them free
- To know that Jesus died on the Cross for their salvation
- To know the love of God that surpasses any brokenness
- To receive forgiveness of sins
- To know that dreams can and do come true

- To know that God can work all things (even bad things) out for good to those who love Him

PREFACE

As an author with Traumatic Brain Injury, it is a miracle that I have been able to write a series such as this. It has been a very long haul of uphill battles, especially with the editing. Having a brain impairment hasn't stopped me from writing. Although this book has been sent out for editing purposes, the final outcome of the editing rests solely with me. It has taken years to bring something of value to the readers of Summer Ray.

Yet, it is still not a perfect work of art. I cannot promise flawless grammar and punctuation, as some of the 19th Century names are spelled for that time period. The format is as close to what my brain can understand. Having a disability, the focus is more on detail, not on format. I can, at the very least make certain, to the best of my ability, I have given my heart and soul into making sure that you, the reader, have an outstanding story that you will cherish for many years to come.

God bless you and thank you for wanting to be a part of our Summer Ray world.

INTRODUCTION

Everyone who has ever written a book on Gettysburg, has his or her own story to tell — whether historical facts or fiction. This book is especially written because of a promise I made, while doing research on Big Round Top on February 1, 2009. This book is not meant to offend the "true historians" of Gettysburg. It is also not meant to offend those who believe in the spiritual side of Gettysburg, who may or may not elaborate on the true historical facts.

I have found, especially in this particular town, one is not supposed to mix historical facts with spiritual reality. However, as an historian and spiritual woman, I found it impossible to discuss one side without the other. This book is where my two worlds collide. So, please bear in mind this book is simply an attempt by the author to keep her promise to Civil War Soldiers, who gallantly fought at the most gruesome historical battle on American soil.

"Summer Ray" is spiritual, historical, paranormal, romantic, and a self-help story, all rolled into one fascinating series. Between the front and back covers is intricately woven a story, within a story. Some of the characters play themselves and are cast with their real names. Of course, all gave me prior permission. I purposely did that to make the Summer Ray Series as real as possible.

The story of Summer Ray is set in her beloved town of Gettysburg. The backdrop is Maryland where she actually lives. Her passion to help the Unknown Soldiers; her love for Jennie Wade and Jack Skelly; her real-life struggles with self-esteem due to injuries; her battle with evil; and sudden life twists and turns; these all give you, the reader, something human and tangible to relate to.

For all of you ghost and paranormal guys and gals reading this story, there are plenty of witches, warlocks, demons and ghosts running around. But for all of you spiritual, bible-believing people, there are plenty of Angels and references to God as well. Last but not least, for all you historians, I can assure you, after several

22

thousand hours of research, I have made sure the *Summer Ray Series* is historically and demographically correct. However, the genre of this book is "Historical Fiction." There are some fictional characters and locations concerning history.

It is my sincere desire that you, the reader, are richly inspired by reading this book and others that follow. It is the heartfelt wish of this author to encourage you to fulfill your purpose and your destiny while here on planet Earth. Should you find yourself blessed by what you are about to read, all glory must go to God and not to me − the author.

And so, let the true, the sort of true, and the not true at all mysterious and captivating story begin...

24

"May the heart of this fair land be forever inclined unto wisdom, so that we may never fall into the folly of another war, and be compelled to pay the fearful penalty that is sure to follow."

Tillie Pierce Alleman

CHAPTER ONE

Kept the Dream Alive

December 23rd

Having caught the Amtrak from Harrisburg, PA at 8:30AM, the passenger train pulled into Penn Station at 11:40AM, on a frigid snowy Friday morning. The New York City station is just below the famous Madison Square Garden in Manhattan and is close to the Grand Central Terminal.

New York City this time of year is more crowded than usual. Tourists by the millions visit the city, just to see the holiday lights or do their Christmas shopping at Macy's, Bloomingdale's or other well-known department stores. Lovebirds like to take a romantic stroll in the moonlight. Starry-eyed, they watch the snow fall by the Statue of Liberty at Ellis Island, in the Hudson River. Some brave folks like to be daring and walk across the illustrious Brooklyn Bridge with all its dazzling lights; while others, as a tradition, like to take the trip to the city just to see the gigantic Rockefeller Christmas tree. This special holiday tree, as a requirement, has to be at least 65 feet tall and 35 feet wide. The present tree stands an enormous 80 feet tall and 50 feet wide, and like most of the other Rockefeller Christmas trees this one is also a Norway spruce.

Of course, some of the awe-struck tourists catch a show at the Radio City Music Hall for their "Christmas Spectacular," featuring those high-kicking, gorgeous Rockettes. Then there are those sneaky and very sweet men. These are the guys that like to surprise their unsuspecting ladies, while ice skating at the Rockefeller ice rink, with a marriage proposal. Though Summer Ray would never admit it, she often dreamed of that herself.

The two middle aged ladies in the yellow cab, stuck in city traffic, none of the above reasons sent for them. Summer Ray Sherwood, a newly 50-year-old author, was dressed in a slick black suit with the skirt well above her knees. Her high heels gracefully adorned those hard-calloused feet of hers. Years of ice skating, having to wear skates a size smaller than her normal shoes, left its mark.

28

Yet, along with her well-manicured nails, her jet-black hair, streaked with a few strands of white was pulled up in a banana clip, other than a few wispy bangs. With the heels, Summer Ray stood 5'8." Her long, muscular legs she never minded showing off. Eyes of golden brown, if one looked deep enough, could see the real reason she was sitting in a cab with her best friend of over forty years.

Kathryn Black, or Kat for short, was Summer Ray's voice of reasoning since the 2nd grade. Summer was impulsive, impatient and suffered from what she referred to as her alphabet issues; Traumatic Brain Injury (TBI); Post Traumatic Stress Disorder (PTSD); Obsessive Compulsive Disorder (OCD) and Attention Deficient Disorder (ADD). A tragic car accident in her earlier years also left Summer Ray with partial hearing loss and at times her mouth could not process what her mind was trying to speak.

Kat, or Katie during school years, on the other hand, was always so darned protective, logical and careful. Summer liked to take chances. Kat, some of those times, had to pick up the pieces of the risks that her

29

best friend took. She was like a human Jiminy Cricket, or perhaps a God-given, human Angel for Summer Ray to lean on.

Kat spoke, "So, here we are again. We are back in your other beloved city." Summer turned to look at her best friend sitting beside her in the back seat and questioned, "Other beloved?"

Kat grinned and said, "Your obsession with Gettysburg, Silly. You know, ever since you were five years old. Duhhh!"

Summer agreed and added with a slight stutter, "Yes! New Yorrrk City is a magical place Kat. I know you aren't one for 'citayyy' traffic. But for some reason it sticks to me." Summer went back to staring out the cab window. Still hating her stutter after all these years, Summer hadn't overcome the "something is wrong with me," kind of thoughts.

Kat responded as if feeling her best friend's longing. She ignored Summer's obvious speech impediment and said, "He's gone Summer Ray. When are you going to get a grip and move on? The General you fell in love with, is gone."

Summer shook her head as if to try and ignore what her best friend had said.

When Kat started singing a Christopher Cross song, something about the moon and New York City, Summer reached over and slightly elbowed her friend. The nice Mexican male cab driver, looking through the rear-view mirror at his passengers smiled, like he had a hidden secret kind of smile. Had the ladies not been so engrossed in their conversation they would have seen his eyes change from a glowing neon blue, to a deep dark brown. Summer sighed as Kat asked, "How can you not fall in love in a city like this?"

Summer replied, "I don't want to fall in love Kat. I just want to know why he disappeared. Don't you get it? I have no closure. I don't know why he left, and I need to know." Summer gestured to her friend with her long freshly painted pink nails.

Kat changed the subject, "Well... in a few minutes we will know why your dad's lawyer summoned us here. At least you can have closure in regard to him."

Summer answered as she fought back tears, "Yes!" Just then, the cabbie interrupted their

31

conversation as he pulled the cab over to a curb, "Here you are ladies!" With the sound of "chi-ching" he continued, "That will be $14.50."

Summer paid the cabbie and said her "Thank you," all the while forgetting to wish him a "Merry Christmas." Luckily, Kat Black was more aware of the season and wished him a "Season's Greetings" from both her and her oblivious friend. The cabbie smiled as they shut the door and he sped off to be waived down by other anxiously awaiting passengers.

Standing in front of the Marshall and Lockheed Building, the ladies looked rather small. The building, after all, had 110 floors. Though Summer's dad's attorney's office was on the 82nd floor, Summer told him she was not about to take an elevator up that high. Her fear of heights prevented her. Mr. Marshall gladly obliged and assured his clients' daughter that he would meet her and Kat on the 1st floor, in a nearby private conference room.

A black door greeter named "Mike," dressed in a black tux, sporting a nicely trimmed white beard, politely tipped his hat as he opened the heavy glass and bronze doors and said, "Good Day Ladies and Happy Holidays." Summer Ray snapped back into reality when she wished the door greeter a "Merry Christmas" in return. Almost forgetting her manners, she then added, "Thank you, Sir." Mike gave her a smile as a sign of his forgiveness. Yet, as soon as Summer took a step up to walk inside the building, she suddenly stopped so fast that Kat ran into her back.

Kat exclaimed, "I wish you would stop doing that or at least give me the five second warning." Summer didn't say a word. She just looked to the right near the stair railing. Her eyes darkened to almost black. Her face hardened like stone as she gave the invisible audience a harsh glare and muttered something under her breath. A confused Mike didn't see a damn thing. But with kindness, he just waited patiently for this rather odd woman to finish her entrance into the building. He continued to hold the not so light door open without complaint.

Kat looked at him and said, "Don't ask. She does this a lot."

Without saying a word, Summer Ray picked up her pace and continued into the building with Kat following not so closely behind her. Instantly, a bright light surrounded them, none apparent to the human eye, of course! Sostar made sure, the creature's preoccupation with the ladies was suddenly squashed.

Upon walking into the plush office building, the very attractive and cordial front desk receptionist Ms. Decklin, alerted Mr. Marshall, Sr. of the ladies arrival.

Mr. Marshall, now in his early 70's, was still a fine looking gentleman. His winter white hair, cobalt blue eyes with just a hint of crow's feet and tall slim stature, made him one of the "Most Eligible Bachelors" in all of New York City. Not to mention the fact, he was slightly rich. But not the extravagant rich like the Trumps.

Yet, he really wasn't a bachelor. He was a widower. His wife of thirty-five years passed away from diabetes. Mr. Marshall hadn't let her go either. He was still married to his wife. His long hours at the office compensated him for the loneliness he would feel at home and for now that was okay with him. Every night after he leaves the office, he walks straight to Alley's grave site, or "The Mrs.," as he came to call her, and tells her about his day. It is a rule he has never broken. No! Not since their first kiss some sixty years ago.

It is true romantic love at its best. It was something Summer Ray longed for, since watching her first real movie, Cinderella. She was only three years old. Summer grew up believing that is how love was supposed to be, and now, at a half a century in age, she still believes in fairytales. It was the coming true part that she had started to have trouble with it. She was very unlucky at love. But the dream of love kept her faith alive that someday, happily ever after would be hers.

Last Wishes

When Summer saw one of her parents' oldest friends, she stood up and walked over to him. No longer able to hold back the tears, she just let them fall. Mr. Marshall hugged his friends' daughter and said, "It is very nice to see you again Summer Ray, although I am terribly sorry it is still under these distressing circumstances. Oh, and I see you have brought Ms. Black, excellent!"

Kat held out her hand to shake Mr. Marshall's and replied, "It is very nice to finally meet you. But I too, wish it were under better circumstances." Mr. Marshall motioned for the ladies to follow him to the waiting Conference Room. As he closed the door behind them, he offered the ladies coffee, tea or just about anything they wanted.

Summer refused and Kat followed her lead. Summer just wanted to get to the matters at hand.

Her father's attorney spoke, "I am sure you both are wondering why I asked you here on this particular day."

Summer affirmed, "I thought we settled my parents' estate last April."

Mr. Marshall assured her, "We did Summer Ray. This has nothing to do with finances. It is more of a personal matter, one your father said that only I could pass along to you." Summer with newly waxed arched eyebrows, gave her best friend a confused look.

Mr. Marshall continued, "Let's get right to the point." He pulled out a small manila envelope from inside his Armani suit jacket and hand delivered it to Summer Ray stating, "Per your father's last wishes, you are to open this letter in front of me and your best friend, Kathryn Black. If you are wondering if I know what it contains, I do not."

Summer crossed her long muscular skating legs, pulled her skirt down just a bit, accepted the envelope, took a deep breath and opened the letter. She did not notice her best friend squirm a little in her seat beside her. Summer was too engrossed in what her father had left for her. Scanning the handwritten letter, from what looked like her aged father's own hand, she began to read out loud.

"My dearest Summer Ray, if you are reading this letter, it is because your mother and I are both now in Heaven. I trust Kathryn is with you to see to it that you are not falling apart.

What I am about to tell you might come as a terrible shock. I was asked to never tell you

37

the truth, but there are some things you just cannot take to the grave with you. I will get right to the point; both you and your brother Greg were adopted."

Summer gasped then continued, "Your mother and I could not have children of our own, and we desperately wanted children. The only other alternative was to adopt. Since your brother died so long ago, it matters not who his birth parents are. But since I trust you will be around at least until you are 100 years old, as determined and as strong willed as you are to stay young, it is only fair you know the truth. If the shock of being adopted wasn't hard enough, what I am about to share with you, is even harder.

Our family history contains men who fought for the Union. To this day, you Summer Ray are still a strong advocate for the Northern Cause. Your love for the Civil War, the Unknown Soldiers, the abolition of slavery and especially Gettysburg, you are a Yankee woman

38

through and through. Be that as it may, you were born in Savannah, Georgia. So, in reality, you are Southern Born, just not Southern Bred."

Summer could barely breathe and put her right hand up to cover her mouth, then removed her hand so she could keep reading,

"Your birth mother is part Cherokee and it explains why you have jet black hair. I know your brother while growing up used to tease you about your hair, telling you that you were adopted. I used to flinch every time he said that for fear you would realize it was the truth. Your birth mother was only 15 years old when she got pregnant with you. Her parents (your maternal grandparents), felt it best she give you up for adoption.

Your birth name is Natasha. But when I first held you in my arms at the age of six weeks old, you lit up my life like the sun. So, we changed your name to Summer Ray. As far as your

39

biological father, we didn't have much information on him, other than he is listed on your original birth certificate. Once we legally adopted you, we were allowed to change it and add my name and your mother's name instead.

All the documents you need are upstairs in my bedroom closet. If you go into the closet and take up the last two floorboards on the right, you will find another box containing them.

So, your heart is asking why your mother and I did not tell you when we were alive. It isn't that we didn't have the guts to tell you. We just both never wanted you to feel that you were any less a part of us. You were and still are 100% our daughter. We didn't want you to feel different. I think it is more of a shock to you finding out that you have a Southern heritage, than it is to find out you were adopted. I believe that Savannah is calling you. I trust as a woman who loves research, you will find your maternal family in no time.

Just know my love for you is never ending. When you see the stars sparkle at night, think of your mother and me shining down on you. I asked you to come to New York City on December 23rd so you could skate at the Rockefeller Center. I had Mr. Marshall make arrangements so you can skate to "O Holy Night." I know it is your favorite song. This is my last request of you. When the doctors said you couldn't skate again after your accident, you conquered all the odds. I know this news is a terrible blow. But I trust the ice will help you heal once again.

May the God I serve lead and guide you as you start this new journey. Kathryn, once again, I trust that you will be there with Summer Ray through it all. You, too, are a daughter to me. I bless you and my beloved grandson, Billy; Kathryn and her family, in the name of the Father, the Son and of the Holy Spirit.

Your Forever Loving, Dad."

Summer, with tears in her eyes as she put the letter on her lap, had no idea her best friend carried that same secret ever since their college days. Kat knew the truth but never disclosed it. The attorney saw the shock on Summer's elegantly made up face, as she suddenly turned a ghostly white. Mr. Marshall got to his feet and asked, "Would you like a few moments alone?" A defiant Summer Ray Sherwood also got to her feet and answered, "No! Mr. Marshall, I am fine!"

Kat stepped in and exclaimed, "Like hell you are! You don't always have to be so brave, you know. You have just been hit by a Mack truck. It is okay to grieve Summer Ray."

Summer turned to her friend and said, "I have already been hit by a Mack truck. I survived. I will survive this too. My dad is right. The ice will help me heal." Summer hugged her dad's attorney and as he opened the door he replied, "Summer Ray, if there is anything you need, please do not hesitate to call me."

Summer simply nodded her head and without emotion walked out the door. Kat on the other hand, stopped to thank Mr. Marshall for fulfilling her best friend's parents' last wishes.

Mr. Marshall firmly spoke, "Make sure she gets to that ice precisely at 7:00PM."

Kat answered, "Of course!" Kat then almost had to run to catch up to Summer. Having carried the burden of truth, of Summer's adoption, revealing her knowledge of it was not something Kathryn Black was looking forward to. Kat sighed and then prayed a small prayer, "Oh God, please give me strength."

Summer stepped out into the flurries of beautiful white snowflakes with Kat following not far behind. Mike, the door greeter, instructed the ladies to watch their step. Summer was in a state of shock and there was nothing Kat could do to help her. The message was clear. Summer's world once again was shattered. Where was the General when Summer needed him the most? Kat thought, "Oh that's right, gone!" Feeling just as helpless as her best friend, Kat walked sadly close by her side. Summer was loudly silent.

Time would eventually be right for Kat to tell her distraught best friend the truth. But it wasn't going to be anytime soon. Because of the feelings of betrayal Kat knew Summer would have, it was best for Kat to stay silent. Kat had to allow her best friend to heal from yet another devastating setback. Yes! Summer's dad knew his daughter all too well. How could she grieve while skating on the most beautiful ice of all surrounded by Christmas music and angels in her midst? Kat was thankful Summer wasn't about to ignore her parents last wishes. She knew, adopted or not, where Summer Ray was going to be at 7:00PM that evening. Kat felt a sense of relief. It was eventually going to be okay and work out for Summer's good.

CHAPTER TWO

O Holy Night

Ever since Summer Ray heard someone singing "O Holy Night" on the radio, her father knew she dreamed of ice skating a program to that song at the Rockefeller Center in New York City. Summer always wanted to re-locate to the city, but she just couldn't bring herself to move away from her dearly loved Gettysburg, or her beloved son, Billy, who still attended college there. Standing at rink side next to her best friend, Kat exclaimed, "See Summer Ray, dreams really do come true."

Summer replied, "Yes! New York City is famous for that."

Summer was dressed in a light blue, sequined skating dress, with a white skating jacket. She shimmered as the lights overhead bounced off of her. A crowd had already gathered as they normally do to watch the skaters. The temperature was a cold thirty-nine degrees and the temperature was falling fast. The stars could be seen twinkling in the far distant night sky. Summer had to admit she was excited. Oh, how she loved New York City. It was for certain her home away from home.

As she entered the ice to warm up, other skaters were happily skating around the rink. Kat opted to stay rink side and not skate. She thought it best to give Summer Ray some time alone on the ice she loved. It didn't matter where the ice was, ice was ice and she was a free spirit while skating on top of it.

In all of the hustle and bustle of the season, Kat failed to notice a strange man taking a spot beside her. When she strained to get a better look at her friend on the ice, she practically stepped on the stranger's boots. Kat caught her breath then offered her apology.

"Oh, I am sorry. I didn't see you standing there." Yet, when she did finally get a good look at him, she couldn't help but admire his beauty. It wasn't just how handsome he looked. There was something more, like an aura around him that drew Kat to him. He smiled and said, "No apology necessary Ma'am. It is rather crowded around here."

46

An appalled Kat grimaced and asked, "Ma'am? Did you just call me Ma'am? Do I look like a Ma'am to you?"

The bemused stranger smiled and answered, "No Ma'am. Sorry, I was brought up this way. So please, do not be offended."

Kat laughed and responded with, "You sound like a Southern gentleman, misplaced in the wrong time period." The man smiled and Kat swooned. Due to his presence, she knew she was melting in the freezing cold. So, she said, "I noticed you are wearing boots. Don't you skate?"

The stranger in a clear Southern voice replied, "I do, but not tonight. I noticed your friend from up above and had to weed my way through the crowd just to find you. Who is she?"

Kat answered, "She is my best friend and she is going through a rough time right now."

He laughed and replied, "Protective, are we?"

Kat said, "Very!" With that both Kat and the stranger looked out at Summer Ray. Her favorite song had begun and she was in her God given glory.

As Summer spun around to do a layback, she couldn't help but look up toward Heaven and the stars that were shining down upon her. Spinning around and around, she gracefully stretched her right arm up to finish the spin. Almost touching the sky, Summer faded into her own little world once again with her, the ice and her God.

Yet as the faces of her parents appeared like stars shining down upon her, just like her father said they would, Summer Ray faded into the memories of days she could no longer remember. With the words to the most beautiful song she has ever heard growing faint, her father's voice was growing louder and louder. As she was being pulled into the vortex of yet another vision, Summer Ray Sherwood let go and finally freed herself from the present-day restraints.

...Forty-five years earlier

CHAPTER THREE

For God and For Country

Summer drifted back to the year 1967. Her dad's sky-blue Oldsmobile was sitting alongside the frozen pond where he took his daughter ice skating in the small town of historical Gettysburg. It wasn't the large frozen lakes he was used to, but it would have to do. John Walter Sherwood or J.W. for short, grew up on ice skates in Ottawa, Canada. At the age of thirty-two, he was still an avid ice hockey player. His parents moved him to the east coast of the United States soon after his 14th birthday.

Summer was wearing her very first pair of double-bladed ice skates. Her dad had hoped his love of the ice, would eventually rub off on his little girl.

"That's right, Summer Ray," J.W. told his five-year-old daughter, "You can do this."

Summer replied back in a broken and scared voice, "But I'll fall."

"No, you won't, Summer. Keep your arms outstretched just like I showed you. Strong arms, Summer Ray. Don't look down or up. Summer, what are you looking at?" her puzzled dad asked.

Summer questioned her dad, "What are those mountains called?"

J.W. looked up at the source of his daughter's curiosity and replied, "Big Round Top and Little Round Top, now please focus. The ice isn't going to stay frozen all year you know. Come on Honey, just skate." John Sherwood instructed his daydreaming daughter.

Summer was relentless and asked, "But what's up there, Daddy?"

Summer's dad turned again to look up at Big Round Top and said, "Snow, Summer snow. Now practice. March, march, glide. That's it. That's my girl."

Summer started marching and gliding across the ice, while peeking back over her right shoulder to look again at Big Round Top and couldn't help but notice a majestic bald eagle hovering over the mountaintop. This was a rarity in Gettysburg. The morning sky was also changing right before her very eyes. The sun had finally crested over the top of the mountains and was beaming through the archway of the castle on Little Round Top.

When Summer first looked up, vivid colors of yellow and orange streaked across the open sky. Sunrays glistened off the snow-covered mountains and reflected off the cannons on Confederate Avenue. Suddenly, the sky turned a deep red and for some unknown reason, the clouds began to display colors of Union Blue and Confederate Gray. Mesmerized, little Summer Ray Sherwood began to hear faint sounds of "The Battle Hymn of the Republic" in what sounded like fifes and drums.

As Summer skated on the frozen pond in Gettysburg, even at the tender age of five years old, she was still fascinated by some of the Civil War stories her dad and grandpa told her. The stories of her great-great grandpa, Union General Richard S. Sherwood were etched in the pages of her mind. These were real life horror stories, of how he spent cruel winters of the Civil War in Tennessee. Her great-great grandpa was indeed a dedicated officer, sharing the suffering and mayhem of the carnage of that brutal war with his regiment.

As Summer kept looking up at Big Round Top, her thoughts faded into the war instead of the matters at hand. Her dad's fainted voice of, "March, march, glide" was strangely replaced with the sights and sounds of Civil War battles...

The Wheat Field; Gettysburg, PA

July 2, 1863

A dirty and dusty Union mail courier on his thoroughbred, made his way to the Wheat Field not far from Big Round Top and saluted a Union Colonel.

"Colonel McDaniels, Sir, I have orders from Brigadier General Barnes," the dispatch rider shouted, after saluting the commanding officer.

The Colonel saluted him back and started reading the orders. The courier then asked, "Colonel, Sir, is there anything further to report back?"

The Colonel replied, "Give my regards to the Brigadier General and tell him we are holding our line."

"Yes, Sir! Oh, I have this for you Colonel, Sir." The courier pulled out a small envelope and continued speaking, "It came a few days ago. It is an urgent letter from your wife."

The Colonel demanded, "A few days ago? Why am I just receiving this now?"

The mail courier stated, "I am sorry, Sir. I was held up by Longstreet. Daisy and I, we had to sneak in from behind that mountain over there." He pointed to Big Round Top.

It was the 2nd day of the Battle of Gettysburg. The Colonel and his men were in position at the rocky wooded crest of the hill, on the Wheat Field. Anderson's Brigade, under Hood's Division, commanded by General Longstreet opened fire on the crest of the hill where the Colonel McDaniels and his regiment were positioned. Under shot and shell, the Colonel's men were mortally wounded, most of them left unrecognizable. These faithful men who fought bravely alongside him lay dying for their country, some with only one last breath to ever be heard again, and it was their mothers' names they spoke of.

With the carnage of body parts of the dead around him, their tattered Union uniforms in pieces, and with the blood of his regiment splattering the Wheat Field, the Union Colonel Michael Moses McDaniels, overcome with loss, cried out in mortal agony to the reality, of the fragility, of human life. For a brief few seconds his thoughts flashed back to happier times when the Colonel had a bright future still yet to be lived.

The Colonel was a fine officer. He was a West Point graduate, born and raised in Valley Forge, Pennsylvania. His greatest hero was none other than General George Washington of the Revolutionary War and the nation's first President. The Colonel, now in his early thirties, had jet black hair with a thick black beard. He was fiercely loyal to the Union, though ill-tempered at times. Still, the only one he loved more than his men was his wife. He met Lily on her parents' horse farm in Valley Forge. He was a young lad, but he was still considered an adult at seventeen years old.

It was love at first sight for the both of them. But, seeing how she was only fifteen when he first laid his eyes on his lady love, her parents made them wait until she was a year older before they could marry. Such beautiful and fond memories, until the roar of the Confederate cannons sadly and viciously interrupted them.

The Colonel's mind, now back on the slaughter surrounding him, wrestled with his actions as a leader. Having an urgent message from his beloved wife, while in battle, was a cause of great distress for him. He had hoped she hadn't taken ill, as he would not be able to leave his post as Colonel. As he anxiously opened the letter to read it, gunfire was heard in the background. Almost blinded by thick black and gray smoke, the Colonel wiped his brow from sweat and smoke and he began to read:

Michael,

I have just divorced you and remarried. Steven is an accountant and he has nothing to do with war. I could not sit here and wait another day, never knowing one day to the next if you would return

57

to me. I couldn't bear the thought of being alone forever. I am sorry to have to tell you this way.

Signed, Lily Andrews

The Colonel knew he only bowed his head for a split second. He would not allow the emotions of that letter distract him from his duty. The Colonel had men to lead and a battle to win. Yet, the moment he put his head back up to issue another order to his men, an artillery shell exploded in the midst of them. This action killed or wounded every living thing within a ten to twenty-yard radius.

At that time, the most agonizing sounds could be heard all around the Colonel from wounded and dying soldiers. Men were torn to pieces by the shrapnel that blew their bodies apart. Blood now saturated the parched ground underneath what once were his men, as body parts and limbs were spewed about on the hot, sun-blistered Wheat Field.

The Colonels' horse, Buttercup, was instantly killed. The Colonel was thrown a good five feet from her.

58

Colonel McDaniels saw sights that no human should ever have had to see and heard sounds that no human should ever have had to hear. As he crawled to his horse, the Colonel Michael Moses McDaniels was fading fast. The only one of his men that he could recognize, though dead, was Union Lt. Colonel George Jameson. His parents named him George after George Washington and Jameson after the James River. The Lt. Colonel often wondered why he wasn't a Confederate with such a Southern name. His is devotion to the Union never let his mind wander too far.

As the Lt. Colonel laid there dead, beside what used to be the Colonel's regiment, the Colonel edged up to Buttercup and with one last bit of strength left, he draped his left arm over what he could of his faithful mare. As the Colonel Michael Moses McDaniels, of the Union Army of the Potomac, breathed his last, he sadly took the blame of his men's death with him, to a solitary and endless grave of despair.

All the sudden, what appeared to be the brightest and the most glorious light he had ever seen flashed all around him. An Angel, descended from the clouds in splendor, stood glowing before him.

The Colonel bemoaned, "How can I go on and find eternal rest, knowing my men are dead because of me?"

Before the Angel could depart from the Colonel, she looked up into the crystal diamonded sky, as if to wait for an answer. Suddenly, what looked like manna from Heaven began to rain down on them. The Angel turned to a now kneeling Colonel, blew on her golden trumpet and then proclaimed,

"Colonel Michael Moses McDaniels, of the Union Army of the Potomac, from henceforth you are named the General of the Confederate and Union Unknowns. It has been granted by God above, to promote you in rank, to watch over the Unknowns and the town of Gettysburg. You must see to it that your heart does not become bitter. A heart full of bitterness creates deadly poison and many are defiled by it and remain in their torment. I shall return to you and to the Unknowns after many days have passed."

The mystified General asked, "The Unknowns?"

Without answering, the Angel lifted her arms and wings toward Heaven and ascended effortlessly into the now cloudless sky, disappearing out of the Colonel's sight. The Angel left in her wake what appeared to be glorious shimmers of gold dust. The Colonel McDaniels, not understanding what the Angel was referring to, suddenly found himself alone on Big Round Top, in a vaporous murky fog. Left alone in his torment, demons from the Underworld were seen taunting and sneering at him.

No, the Colonel was not in Hell, at least not the real one. The only hell he was now living in was the one inside his soul. Which for the tormented, could seem like the real thing. How long would he be sentenced to this prison-like torture of unrest? No one but God knew, as the Colonel self-sentenced himself.

Still, the once Colonel of the Union Army of the Potomac, now to the United States Unknowns, Confederate or Union, he became the General. It was an assignment Michael Moses McDaniels was not necessarily ready to bear. After all, some of those Unknowns were Confederates. He fought against them and was even responsible for some of their deaths and vice versa. Now, it was his lot to watch over them until peace could be obtained. Yet where these mysterious Unknowns were, had yet to be revealed.

The General, long after the 19th Century, kept trying to justify his actions for wanting to stay behind. But the Unknowns who fought alongside the Colonel and the Unknowns who came to serve under him as the General, knew it was nothing more than his pride. The demise of his men was not due to his lack of leadership.

When Ariel, the Angel of Welcome, came for the Unknowns, one by one they would take a knee indicating they did not want to leave their General. It was like watching something from an ice hockey game. If a player got hurt, regardless of what team they played on, the players on both teams would take a knee until the injured player was safely removed from the ice. The United States Unknowns, out of loyalty to God and country, had no intentions of leaving their General, until he too could be safely removed from the bonds that held him.

Every time the Unknowns received permission from the Angel to remain as they were, back at The Gettysburg National Cemetery, the number or word "Unknown" on each of their tombstones was set ablaze, in what looked like a fiery glow of radiation. As Angelic rays of gold dust ascended from the blazing numbers and the inscribed words "Unknown," formations of the numbers and words appeared six feet above each marker. While these formations hovered over each marker, they transformed into the Unknown soldiers' names, rising toward the sky. Heaven knew the name of the mangled bodies or bones that rested underneath those stones, even if the rest of the world did not. God certainly did. It was His divine grace recognizing each individual soldier by name who was buried there.

The phenomenon did not stop at the cemetery. Out on the open battlefields, all across Gettysburg flickers of light sparkled. This was due to the remains of soldiers, whether Union or Confederate, still buried beneath the blighted landscape. Some people thought they saw lightning bugs or orbs and did not bother to take a second glance. Yet, there was someone in particular who actually waited for the event to take place and having waited close to 80 years, the wait was unpredictably over.

The Gatekeeper

At the 10:00PM curfew over at the National Cemetery, the old gatekeeper was out providing his regular rounds of maintenance, removal of spent flowers and trash cleanup. He, along with the Gettysburg Park Rangers, are the only individuals allowed on park property at that time of night. Anyone caught in the cemetery, breaking curfew, would receive a massive and whopping fine of $10,000 dollars. As the faithful old gatekeeper reached down to pick up some trash on the walkway, in front of the figure of Peace, on the Genius of Liberty's statue, something flashed out of the corner of his eye. He then suddenly dropped what was in his hands and witnessed in awe the beautiful, majestic, Angelic gold dust formations, hovering in the air surrounding him.

Overcome with wonder at the marvelous sight, The Gatekeeper, frozen in the place in which he stood, did not dare make a sound or move. He was witnessing a once in a lifetime occurrence, the possible finality of the Unknowns resting in peace. How he knew this, was due to "The Gatekeepers Log" that passed the secret down from one generation to the next, since the first of the Civil War dead were interred.

The old gatekeeper immediately smiled and looked up toward Heaven, intently watching as the golden names were lifted up above the treetops. When the gold dust suddenly began to dissipate and sprinkle on the cemetery like fireworks, the gatekeeper was suddenly sad. He knew that meant the Unknowns had rejected once again Heaven's offer of eternal rest. Why they did that, not one of the gatekeepers could answer.

It was a mystery that carried over into the 21st Century, where planes and flying men to the moon and back were never even looked upon as possible in the 19th Century. The President of The United States of America in the year 2012 was President Barack Obama. Back in the year 1863, it was President Abraham Lincoln. Both

65

Presidents were Commanders in Chief during war time. Lincoln's brief celebration of winning the war for the Union was savagely short lived. Sadly, only five days after General Lee's army surrendered to General Grant at Appomattox, Lincoln was assassinated on April 14, 1865 at Ford's Theatre in Washington, D.C.

History brings with it such conflicting emotions, theories and opinions. It mattered not what Summer Ray was told about her President, be it Lincoln or Obama. She would never stray from the country she loved, nor from the Union she was so passionate about, as President Abraham Lincoln was her second most cherished president. Like the General McDaniels, her first love was President George Washington. Yet, heaven help the Confederate who talked bad about her beloved Abe. Her eyes would flash, her brows would bend, and her lack of self-control would cause her to rant and rave about a President who had long since been departed.

General McDaniels was in desperate need of redemption. Summer Ray was in desperate need of compassion toward those "damn Rebels" and "traitors of the Union," as her grandpa called them. She also deemed the Confederates unworthy of her time and attention. But isn't it just like God to create an answer of resolution out of His love and mercy?

As the General was lost in his ever-increasing bitterness, almost a century and a half later, the absolution was forthcoming. Summer Ray was consumed in her own world of figure skating competitions, college, her view of the world, past and present, and her ever increasing disdain and contempt of the Confederacy. Yet, the moment would soon arrive when her world would unexpectedly be forever challenged and most definitely transformed and altered, whether Summer Ray Sherwood liked it or not.

Sixteen years later...

CHAPTER FOUR

A Road to Gettysburg

Sitting on Summer Ray's queen size poster bed, on top of her patch-quilt comforter and surrounded by stuffed animals, Katie watched as Summer filled up her backpack with her camera, notebook and other odds and ends. Summer's long, jet-black hair was in pigtails, underneath a pale blue knit cap her grandmother knitted for her. Katie's shoulder length wavy red hair, on the other hand, was almost as fiery as her mood.

"Come on, Summer Ray, it's the middle of winter and the Tops are full of ice and snow!" Katie scolded her.

Summer, in her defense replied, "I have to go Katie. I don't know why it has to be today. It just does. Are you with me or not?"

Katie tried to reason with Summer, "You KNOW how dangerous it is up there, even for you, Summer Ray. You might be an experienced figure skater. You are not, however, an accomplished mountain climber, ESPECIALLY not in these weather conditions."

"Come on, I'll get you a Café Mocha Latte." Summer pleaded. Katie sighed in defeat. As Summer finally coerced her friend into making the trek to the Tops, she threw her backpack over her left shoulder.

Katie demanded, as she jumped off the bed, "It better be an extra-large." Summer was twenty-one years old, a senior in college studying journalism and history. One of her final papers for graduation consisted of writing a thesis on a major battle and she just couldn't think of a better battle than that of her beloved Gettysburg. Summer lived in northern Maryland only thirty minutes from Gettysburg. She attended Mt. Saint Mary's College, where her dad was also an alumnus. Starting at the tender age of five years old, her dad used to take her ice skating at a pond on a horse farm in Gettysburg. Back then, the winter was cold enough to actually freeze the ponds.

The month of February in Pennsylvania usually brought with it a lot of heavy snow and at times, sleeting rain and ice. This year was no different. Regardless,

Summer was incredibly adventurous and highly motivated. She wasn't concerned about the dangers of going to the Tops in the ice and snow. Summer just wanted to go. Or rather, she just knew she had to go. It was one of those convictions, or premonitions, that burned inside her. Summer Ray was going to the Tops, come hell or high water. However, she inwardly and secretly hoped neither would be the case.

As Summer Ray and Katie went into the living room of Summer's parents' split-level house, Summer stopped to kiss her dad on top of his balding head, and to grab some Planters peanuts off of the coffee table. John Sherwood was watching an NFL football game, between the Washington Redskins and the New York Giants.

Summer jokingly said, "My Giants are going to rock your Redskins, Dad."

When Summer's dad saw that his daughter and Katie were about to leave the house he cried out, "Hold on, young lady, just where do you think you are going? Kathryn, where is she dragging you off to now? Do you see the roads?"

Summer said, "Dad, Katie and I are driving to Gettysburg."

This time when Summer's dad spoke, he was no longer sitting in his recliner. Even their black lab Smokey, ran for the hills as he saw his master getting up from the chair. John Sherwood sounded more scared than strict when he exclaimed, "What? In this weather? Oh no you are not, young lady!"

He turned to speak to Katie saying, "Kathryn, you're supposed to be the level headed one in the bunch."

Katie defended herself and replied, "I tried to tell her, but as usual, she just wouldn't listen."

A determined Summer enlightened her worried dad, "I am an adult. You know I am going with or without your permission."

Knowing he couldn't stop her, Summer's dad reluctantly gave in and replied,

"Okay Summer Ray! Since you are so stubborn, take the Blazer, not that piece of crap you call a car."

An overly anxious and hurried Summer answered, "Hey, you helped me to buy it remember.

74

We've got to get going. I need your keys, Dad." As she reached her hand out to receive the car keys, she told her dad, "I am not stubborn. I am strong willed."

Katie laughed and asked, "What's the difference? Your dad is right. If you won't listen to me, at least listen to him. The roads...."

Summer cut her off with a "Hush will you!" No! It wasn't a question, and Summer did not wait for her best friend to answer.

As J.W. dug in his pockets to retrieve the SUV keys, he informed the girls, "If I don't hear from you in an hour, I am sending out a search party. Do you hear me Summer Ray? Kathryn make sure she calls me."

"Yes, Dad!" Katie answered him.

Summer's dad reminded her, "Be careful up there and don't tell your mother Summer. She will have my hide!"

When Summer's dad was finished speaking, he opened the front door for the girls. Summer instantly stopped and stared off into space for a few seconds. She shook off that feeling of darkness and kept on walking out the front door.

Then almost as if in a fog, she slowly turned around and said, "Send Angels, Dad. I think that would be best. They would be better than a search party."

Both Katie and Summer's father looked at each other baffled, as if Summer Ray unconsciously knew something bad or mysterious was about to happen. The girls climbed in the SUV parked in the garage while Summer's dad silently prayed, "Father God, please keep my little girl and Kathryn safe. You know how impulsive my Summer Ray is. She has been obsessed with those Tops since she was five years old. Please send your Angels to guard and to protect them. Thank You! In Jesus Name...Amen."

The Ten Roads

The road conditions getting to Gettysburg, driving up 15 North into Pennsylvania, were actually pretty normal. Summer's dad let them use his four-wheel drive, as he knew his little girl would not take "No!" for an answer. Summer was head strong and strong willed. If the Tops were what she wanted to write about, the Tops is where she would end up, one way or another. Her practical father thought, "It was better to be safe than sorry."

Still trying to make himself feel better, he reasoned, "At least with a four-wheel drive, they will have a better chance of not getting stuck!"

Though no longer a Catholic, Summer Ray still loved to see the golden statue of Mother Mary. She stands high above Mt. Saint Mary's College, located in the Catoctin Mountains in Emmitsburg, Maryland and only a few miles from the Pennsylvania state line.

Summer looked over at her best friend in the passenger seat and said, "Mother Mary always looks so peaceful, like she is watching over us."

Katie replied back to Summer, "Wow! The scenery is breathtaking with her surrounded by all that snow on the mountain."

Kathryn Black was a year older than Summer Ray and also a senior in college. Katie was a beautiful Irish girl, shorter in height than Summer Ray. Though

Katie was a white woman, she had ancestors that were black. Katie's great - great grandparents were slaves in the South. Her family migrated North after the Civil War. They still faced incredible hardships as most blacks did during that time period. Her grandparents knew the famous Dr. Martin Luther King Jr.

Katie's grandfather was at the Mall when he delivered his famous "I Have A Dream" speech. Though Katie was not as passionate about Gettysburg as Summer Ray, she was a godsend for her. Katie was level-headed, stable and not impulsive like Summer. Katie was studying to be an RN at Hood College in Frederick, Maryland not far from Summer's college in Emmitsburg. Summer and Katie grew up together and vowed to someday get married to the love of their lives, live in the same neighborhood and raise their kids together.

Not realizing they had already crossed the Pennsylvania state line, Katie looked down at the map, jumped up from her seat and said, "Take this exit – Steinwehr Avenue. When you get to the top of the ramp, take a left. While on this road, we will be passing Boyds Bear Country and The Eisenhower Hotel & Conference

Center. The road we need to get to the Tops is Confederate Avenue and will be on the right." As Summer began to pull off the road into a car auction parking lot, she was confronted with Katie's apprehension when she asked, "Why are we stopping?"

Summer lightheartedly informed her friend, "Look at the roads, Katie and just think there are ten of them. I have to put us in four-wheel drive. You don't want us getting stuck up here now do you?"

A frustrated Katie asked Summer, "Ten what? Ten plows, ten snowflakes, ten...."

Summer Ray had spent many long hours studying American Sign Language, and at times it would unconsciously appear when she was explaining things. This was one of those times.

Summer began to speak, "There are ten roads that lead into Gettysburg. Those ten roads are part of the reason the battle was accidently started here. General Lee wanted all his men to convene to the Cashtown Gap area, west of Gettysburg and east of Chambersburg. But in order to get to Cashtown, the Confederate armies coming from York, Carlisle and Harrisburg had to pass through the town of Gettysburg. On July 1, 1863, approximately at 7:30AM, a Yankee soldier by the name of Lieutenant Marcellus Jones of the 8th Illinois Volunteer Cavalry, took a shot at a mounted Confederate officer as a Confederate Infantry crossed Marsh Creek and so the battle of Gettysburg had begun."

Summer went on and on about the war, when Katie interrupted her and said, "Wow! You ARE obsessed with Gettysburg. Girl, you need to get a life."

Summer grinned as she jokingly replied, "Yeah well, if I don't get us into four-wheel drive, neither of us may not have a life to get."

As Summer put the SUV in four-wheel drive, she shuddered as if a dark eerie presence just descended upon them.

Katie, seeing her friend's reaction finally spoke up and said, "What is it, Summer Ray? What do you see? You acted like that at your house. You are really starting to freak me out."

"I don't see anything. I just have this feeling like something bad is about to happen, or something bad already happened. Oh, I need to call my dad to let him know we are here."

Summer acted as if the something bad was no big deal.

But Katie didn't let it go and asked, "Should we turn around?"

Summer told her now worried friend, "No Katie. I am beginning to think this is more than a dissertation. This is an assignment from God. Just pray I am right, or we both will be in a whole lot of ugly."

Katie responded, "Thanks! I think I will go throw up now."

Upon seeing Katie's green expression, Summer immediately said, "Uh, not in my dad's brand-new Blazer. He will kill us both, if whatever is out there doesn't kill us first." Seeing Katie eyes almost bulge out of her head, Summer laughed and assured her friend, "I'm kidding. I'm kidding. Geez Katie, calm down."

As Summer pulled out of the car auction parking lot, that strange and eerie sense washed over Katie as well. She began to feel a mysterious presence, much like the one Summer felt. It was almost as if a dark shadow was looming above them and Katie could feel it in her veins. Summer was not clairvoyant or a psychic. She was however, a prophet and a seer who saw visions and was spiritually aware and sensitive – most of the time. Katie on the other hand was into the paranormal, seeing ghosts and spirits.

Summer knew she needed to get to the Tops. Yet, a spirit of anxiety had suddenly engulfed her, like something horrible was about to happen. But fearful that Katie would make her turn around, she stayed silent and hoped her facial expressions and voice did not expose her true emotions. Little did Summer know, Katie felt the same dark eerie presence and decided it was best to keep quiet herself.

The Perfect Solution

Anyone who has ever driven on one of the ten roads leading into Gettysburg, observing the Gettysburg National Military Park, must have the same permeating sensations that they are on sacred ground. It just cannot be helped. The sanctity is in the air. Yet to see the snow-covered battlefields, where so much blood was spilled, gives off a different kind of emotion. It's as if the snow turns the reality of the war into a tranquil and peaceful dream of something so surreal, one can only wonder how the brutality of the Civil War at Gettysburg ever existed.

With the gates to the park open, the drive down Confederate Avenue toward the Tops was a slow one. The road was not plowed and was covered in at least three inches of snow. It was hard to see the road. But a restless Summer didn't care. Her determination overshadowed her sense of caution and she entered the park at her own risk. Still, the ice-covered trees with the sun glistening through them, it looked more like they were witnessing a Disney movie.

Summer said to Katie, "The only thing missing is an outdoor skating rink."

Katie shot back at Summer, "Yeah right! And as you skate on top of a dead soldier's remains, make sure you give him my best regards."

83

"Fine!" Summer hated it when her friend was right and gave her one of those looks. Then said, "What about an indoor ice rink outside of the park? It's a good idea and you know it, Katie. The town wouldn't have to shut down during the winter. I mean, look around you. Do you see anyone on this road other than the two of us? Driving up and down Steinwehr Avenue, did you see people flocking to the town because they just couldn't wait to get here? What about the stores that close December thru March? What about the people who get laid off? Wouldn't an ice rink be the perfect solution to prevent that from happening? We could call it, 'The Gettysburg Gardens Ice Arena'."

Katie looked at her friend with a strange look and asked, "We? What's with the we? Can *we* at least graduate college first?"

Summer smiled then went back to talking about her beloved ice skating. Once Summer started talking about ice, it was almost impossible to get her to stop. So, Katie stepped in and said, "Yes, Summer. It would be the perfect solution. Hockey and figure skating are, after all, winter sports." Katie had to agree.

Big Round Top

When Summer pulled the SUV to the bottom of Big Round Top, she could hardly believe her eyes. Unseen by the girls, sneering at her and Katie through the beauty of the snow-covered landscape up at Devil's Kitchen, or Mini Devil's Den as some call it, on Big Round Top, were large and small creatures of the Underworld, wondering what their "enemy," the Lord, was up to. The Prince of Darkness, Woeburn was thrashing about on the boulders of Devil's Den. He demanded Dogwood, a lesser demon, to scout out these two parasites called humans.

Summer was astonished at the winter wonderland. Icicles hung from the trees and the snow was glistening and shimmering. Miss Summer Ray Sherwood was awestruck. Still, as glorious as the scenery was, Summer's first thought upon seeing the steep slant and the rocks poking through the snow was, "How stupid is this?"

Looking up at Big Round Top, there was about two feet of snow on the ground and from the looks of the trees there was also a lot of ice. Although Summer Ray was a figure skater, she became suddenly aware of what her friend Duane Stone once warned her, "The Tops were no place for mistakes."

Summer told Katie not to come up the hill with her. She really didn't want her best friend to get hurt. If Summer was unexpectedly injured, then at least Katie could get help. Neither of them knew what the feeling of anxiety or premonition that washed over the both of them meant. It was times like these Summer actually came face to face with the consequences of her impulsivity and always after the fact, not before. Katie understood. She loved her friend and was still supportive, but was relieved when Summer told her to, "Stay put."

Katie agreed whole heartedly and replied, "I intend to. Just leave me the keys. While you are up on that hill FREEZING, I can stay in here all nice and toasty."

Summer thought she was only teasing when she said, "If you see me tumbling down the hill, you know like Jack and Jill, at least being a nurse or almost a nurse, you can make sure I don't die!"

Katie replied to her friend, "This is no time for rhymes, Summer Ray. Seeing how those slopes look, me making sure of anything at this point is a very tall order."

Summer grudgingly agreed and said, "Yeah, I know. So, please make yourself useful and start praying."

Unseen to the human eye, there was a phenomenal commotion going on. Angels were high above the treetops in midair flight, while some were sitting on the Pennsylvania Monument on Hancock Avenue, not far from Big Round Top. They were awaiting their orders from Captain Talhelm, a mighty majestic Angel. At eight feet tall in stature and with his blonde hair, eyes of gold and gigantic wing span of nearly thirty feet in diameter, the Captain was indeed, a powerful angelic being to behold.

Foul, demonic spirits were hovering back and forth from Big Round Top to Devil's Den, back to Devil's Kitchen. They could see the increase in angelic activity, and were abuzz with anxiety and reeked of fear. The ghost spirits Union Colonel Michael Moses McDaniels and his Union Lt. Colonel George Jameson on Big Round Top were also aware of the spiritual activity. They both wondered who these two young women sitting at the bottom of the hill were. Hundreds of thousands of tourists flock to Gettysburg each year, quite possibly reaching millions. Yet, neither the Colonel nor the Lt. Colonel, or the frantic sinister spirits, had ever seen this kind of spiritual awaking before by the angelic beings. Summer Ray and Katie were oblivious to all of it.

The weather was crystal clear just cold. The sky was a brilliant bright blue. It was an afternoon trip when the sun was at its highest. Of course, Summer being Summer, did not dress as well as she should have. She was simply too impulsive and too reckless for her own good! Her first attempt up the hill proved to be rather funny. She kept sliding back down. At one point, she tumbled and crashed right into a nearby monument.

A bewildered Union Lt. Jameson asked, "What is she trying to do Colonel, Sir?"

The Colonel huffed, "I do not know!"
He wasn't in much of a mood for games. The Colonel looked down the hill at this clumsy woman trying to make it up a man's hill, or so *HE* believed, and growled, "The

Tops are no place for women, especially not such a scrawny looking one as this!"

The Colonel McDaniels was egotistical, bitter and did not like the sight of any woman on *HIS* hill. When Summer finally reached the summit, the Colonel passed by her in a puff of white smoke that sent shivers down her spine. Not able to see the smoke, Summer could feel however, the arctic chill of this angry ghost named Michael Moses McDaniels.

Summer said to herself, "Get a grip. It's the middle of winter. You are going to get a cold chill." Her own pep talk encouraged her to continue her exploration. She was in search of one of the 20th Maine's Monuments and wasn't far from finding it. The famous Union Colonel Joshua Chamberlain and the 20th Maine Regiment, on July 2, 1863, formed the line of the extreme left and repelled the attack of the Confederate's extreme right of Longstreet's Corps. Along the ridge, breastworks were built by the Union soldiers to protect them from the advancing Confederates. Chamberlain was deemed a hero as his unit ran out of ammunition and they charged with their bayonets instead.

89

The Aftermath
of the Battle of Gettysburg

It was due to the brutality of the Battle of Gettysburg that some of the soldiers who fought there were trapped between two dimensions. Their wounds were just too deep, too painful, and too sad for some of them to find everlasting and eternal peace. Many of these soldiers died alone on the battlefield with no one beside them. Thousands of them died as Unknowns. Union and Confederate Soldiers, sworn enemies, were buried together. They were simply too unrecognizable for anyone to identify them. *They may have died as enemies, but were buried as brothers.*

Yet Summer still grieved over the mass Confederate graves she still visited regularly on top of Culp's Hill. Although they were the enemy, they were still human beings who deserved to be treated with the utmost respect upon their death. When Summer heard that after the war farmers used to throw trash over top of the Confederate mass graves as a sign of disrespect, even as a Yankee woman she was outraged. Some of the

Confederates are still buried on other Union soil, though only God knows where.

On Stony Hill, near the Wheat Field, and all over Gettysburg for that matter, dead Confederate Soldiers were left to rot in the hot, summer sun. Without a proper burial, and without blessings of peace for the hereafter, it is no wonder the blood of these soldiers still cries out for justice in a foreign land. Many Confederate soldiers died of blood loss and/or infection. Though there were Confederate field hospitals, once the Confederate Soldiers retreated, the Confederate Soldiers who were too wounded to move were left behind in Gettysburg. Yet, with war comes atrocities and carnage. The town of Gettysburg attended to their own wounded and dying Union Soldiers first.

With Confederate Soldiers slowly dying on the battlefield, and in some cases, field hospitals, it took days, sometimes even weeks to retrieve the bloated and decomposing bodies from the blighted landscape. The scourge of those horrendous acts has never been wiped clean. Tillie Pierce Alleman once wrote:

"But oh! The horror and desolation that remained. The general destruction, the suffering, the dead, the homes that nevermore would be cheered, the heart-broken widows, the innocent and helpless orphans! Only those who have seen these things, can ever realize what they mean."[1]

While some of the Confederates are marked "Unknown" or with numbers in The Gettysburg National Cemetery, they are often mistaken for Union soldiers. Other more recognizable, fallen Confederates were removed and transferred to Richmond to be buried. The rest, the "lucky ones," were retrieved by their grieving families, and were interred farther South in a family plot.

The remains of so many fallen soldiers, regardless of rank, met the same ghastly fate whether Union or Confederate. They died as enemies. Yet, it is an historical fact, some of them were buried as brothers. How do you identify the remains of such a mangled mess? It was a grueling job, to say the least. After the battle, the sickening stench of death that filled every square inch of air in the town of Gettysburg, almost made breathing impossible. Had preparation for the shock of the aftermath been allotted, it is feasible to say that no amount of research, training, instructions, or advice, could have ever properly prepared the townspeople of Gettysburg for such horrible and grisly conditions.

Makeshift hospitals surrounded the town, as cries of the dying and wounded rang out. Amputations! Oh God, the amputations! Saws, knives and the sound of broken and crushed bones being severed from that of a wounded soldier, as their lifeless limbs were carried away in horse-drawn wagons to be burned outside the town. Can one even imagine in the 21st century, what a sight that was - Union and Confederate hands, feet, and legs, the limbs they were once attached to soldiers as they trotted away in piles? How unspeakably horrific! Confederate soldiers treated like animals, left to fend for themselves, while flies, buzzards and other animals fed from their gaping wounds. Dead and dying Union and Confederate soldiers, baking in the hot summer sun! Words escape even the most eloquent of writers, as there are simply none to express the suffering.

Yet, for some of these soldiers who gave their lives fighting for whatever "cause" they believed in, a proper burial was not to be. It is not possible to "rest in peace" when the preacher doesn't even know your name. Although it is true that the American government has gone to great lengths in honoring these fallen soldiers, the government cannot fix or heal a lost soul, torn between the reality of this dimension and the next. They can only fly flags at half-staff, march in front of the Tombs of the Unknown Soldiers and erect tall statues in honor of those who died. Still, the tormented souls can find no rest. It is a tragedy in and of itself.

The Blood

When Summer finally climbed to the peak of Big Round Top, she was rather proud of herself. If she was afraid, she didn't show it. Summer was too caught up in the history she so dearly loved.

"The rocks," she thought, "are huge!"

Upon her ascent up the hill she read each memorial the best she could, as they were all covered in snow. Once at the top of the hill, she pulled out her note pad and began to jot down some notes on the Tops. Had she seen the thousands of pairs of haunted and glorious eyes looking at her, she would have had a much greater story to write about and a much more fascinating one, to say the least! However, there was no wind, no sound, no odor, no nothing - just a passing chill. But nothing like some of the ghost stories she had read so much about.

In fact, Summer did not believe in ghosts, at least not the fictional ghosts like Casper and some of the Gettysburg ghosts she had read about. She did, however, believe in the devil, fallen angels and disembodied demons. She was a Christian, though not religious. Summer stayed away from psychics, mediums and horoscopes, the reason being simply because fortune telling and witchcraft are both strictly forbidden by God. Though Summer understood the confusion of some, as the gift of prophecy is God inspired, the gift of divination is a gift given by Satan.

To some, the Gettysburg Ghosts are nothing more than folklore for entertainment purposes. To others, the Gettysburg Ghosts are a way of life. Many stories have been told about those who have had actual encounters with these ghostly apparitions. Yet to some, it is all complete and total hogwash, and a dreadful mark on the community. To Summer Ray, all this "ghost stuff" is an abomination to the God she serves. Her best friend, Katie, was much more opened-minded.

Summer Ray grew up in a house of witchcraft, which possibly tainted her mind to the possibility that all this "ghost stuff" could actually be true. Summer's mom was one of those witches, a "White Wicca Witch" in fact. Some call psychics "witches" and some witches are called "psychics." It didn't matter to Summer Ray. She would have nothing to do with it. Summer thought to herself, "There is no such thing as a White Witch. A witch is still a witch, White or Black they all work for the same devil.

What is so sad is that the White Witches, most of them, do not understand they are deceived. They really think they receive their "powers" from God. The Black Witches know they are Satanists. They are deceived into believing that in the afterlife, they will rule and reign with him. Little do they know that when they die without Christ as their Savior, the demons will drag their souls, bound in chains, to Hell. The devil will use them and the White Witches as entertainment, torturing them for all eternity. They will be ridiculed, laughed at, scoffed at and tormented by the devil and his demons. The Underworld will never cease to be amused at their victims' horror, for the choices those "little vermin," as the dark powers like to call them, made of their own free will while alive on planet Earth.

Make no mistake - the devil hates humans! He has no intention of sharing his kingdom with anyone. This is the same devil who tried to kick God off of *HIS* own throne. Do you honestly think the devil would share his hellish throne with a mere human? A mere mortal who he considers to be nothing more than a parasite? Humans replaced the devil and the fallen angels who were once called, " *The sons of God.*"[a] Those who have accepted Christ as their Lord and Savior are now called, "T*he sons and daughters of God.*"[b] No! The devil has no intention of sharing his reign with any human creature.

97

His only intention is to take as many lost souls to Hell as possible. If they are in Hell, they are out of Heaven and away from the God he detests. The gates of Hell open every second, to welcome another new soul into it who can never escape.

Summer wasn't in Gettysburg to find a ghost. She was there to find some answers. However, with the possibility that she was summoned there by the *SPIRIT*, the questions kept changing. Not only did she want to know where the Confederates charged the hill from near the valley below, she also wanted to know where the Union soldiers fought from. There were so many different accounts as to which Top they were actually on. Some historians and tour guides said, they couldn't have fought from Big Round Top because there were too many rocks and trees.

Historians, movie makers and other locals said, they did. But, it didn't stop Summer Ray from doing her own research. She wanted to try to find her own answers and come up with her own conclusions.

Although she really wanted to look out over the rocks to see the snow-covered valley below, it really was just too treacherous. Summer may have been ambitious but was definitely not so stupid she would put her life in danger. So, she walked up to the overlook as far as she could, not seeing the look of disgust on the Colonel's face. She was on the Tops and felt like she was a part of history.

After a little while, she could hear Katie screaming at the top of her lungs, "Summer Ray, where are you? Are you okay?"

Summer sighed and said, "That truly is what middle names are for. Because only when I am being yelled at does someone use it!"

Listening intently nearby, the Lt. Colonel informed his superior officer, "Her name is Summer Ray. Colonel, Sir."

The Colonel, pretending not to notice or hear what his subordinate said to him, noticed Summer Ray all right. He noticed she was a female on his hill and that was enough of a nuisance for him.

As Katie's voice interrupted the serene beauty and stillness that had enveloped Big Round Top in the newborn snow, Summer was spellbound until the frigid reality crept into her fingers and toes. It was at that moment she decided it was best to begin her descent down the hill. As she stepped carefully over this rock and that rock, this branch and that branch, she lost her balance. To her dismay, her feet flew out from under her. It was not the horizontal rink surface that she was accustomed to. Therefore, it was time to grab the closest solid object to prevent her from actually tumbling down Big Round Top and avoid possible trauma or death.

With arms stretched out, desperately trying not to hit her head on either rock or frozen ground, her right hand latched quickly on to a branch that finally broke her fall. While grasping the branch, she screamed out in agony and terror, as thorns dug deep into her skin, slashing open the tender flesh between her right thumb and index finger. Her blood splattered the white snow with crimson red.

"In the middle of winter?" she wailed! Not just at the shock of her fall and injured hand was she gasping, but at the ridiculous sight of thousands of tiny white blossoms between the sporadic thorns.

Summer shrieked out in even more pain as she had to remove the thorns. Upon hearing Summer scream, Katie began to scramble up the hill, only to slide back down it too. When Summer looked down at her hand, blood was gushing out of the cuts where the thorns viciously dug into her. When she looked down at the snow, something mystical was taking place all around her.

The Vision

On the snow-covered ground, Summer caught a glimpse of her own blood. It suddenly traveled across the entire stark white slope, like the veins of a leaf sprawled out. Something happened! As her blood seeped through the snow it mingled with the Civil War Unknowns. The web of Summer's blood supernaturally crossed the dimension of time and space. Like splintering ice on a semi frozen pond, the blood could be witnessed not only by Summer, but by all the Gettysburg Unknowns, both Union and Confederate, below the surface of snow. It was evident to the Colonel, Summer was not just another tourist.

To her astonishment as her splattered blood began to streak across the frozen landscape, under the ice silhouettes of soldiers began to take a ghostly shape as the ground beneath her began to tremble. Summer, as if she was then looking through a vortex, caught a glance of the battle as it was taking place right around her. She saw soldiers drop to their deaths from the shots fired at them. As she heard the cannons and the gunshots, immediately Summer held her hands to her ears, even her wounded hand, to try to drown out the sound, as a now curious Colonel looked on.

All at once, Summer could see the valley below, known as "The Valley of Death," covered in Union and Confederate blood. She could hear the agony of men and what looked like young boys, as they cried out in absolute anguish and suffering. Summer witnessed the carnage of limbs and other body parts as they were blown off of a Union or Confederate soldier. She observed horses dying with flies already hovering over them and the bodies of the dead that lay crushed beneath their once trusted steeds. She could hear the loved ones' of these soldiers – mothers, fathers, wives, sons, daughters, sisters, brothers and friends, - bewailing their safe return. When Summer Ray heard some of the wounded and dying soldiers whisper the names of their beloveds, it was more than she could bear.

Dangerously close to running toward the soldiers during a hailstorm of bullets and artillery shells, in an attempt to try and help them, one Confederate officer in particular caught Summer Ray's foot and tripped her. This action shielded her and kept her from getting hit by shrapnel from the cannons or rifle fire as they volleyed overhead. But this unselfish act of bravery cost him his own life. As this gallant Southern gentleman lay dying in Yankee territory, with his last ounce of strength, he reached into his haversack and handed Summer Ray a pocket watch. As blood was seeping out his lips, she faintly heard him whisper, "Do not let her have it."

Summer, not understanding what this soldier meant, cradled his broken and bloodstained body in her arms. While her tears fell down across his face, "Dixie" in the most beautiful harmonic tune, amazingly enough,

103

drowned out the horrendous sounds of battle. For a split second in time, it was just Summer Ray Sherwood and this dying Confederate officer. She didn't care if he was the enemy. He was a man — a human being with eyes so sad she could barely stand it.

Not able to voice any more last words, he softly hummed the tune of "Dixie" and drifted off to the other side...eternity. As he breathed his last, Summer started crying hysterically and began to lose her own state of consciousness. The vision had caused her to become part of the time and place she was witnessing. As she was immersed in the Civil War past, Summer was losing all sense of her own present-day reality.

"She is going under Colonel, Sir!" gasped the Lt. Colonel Jameson. Worried that this puzzling woman would be forever trapped between two worlds as they were, the Colonel immediately reached out to jar Summer by grabbing her right hand away from her ear. He then covered her blood-stained right hand with a mound of ice-cold snow. This he knew would cause Summer to jolt back into her own present state of consciousness.

Meanwhile, the Union and Confederate Unknown Soldiers, from whence they fell and from where they were buried, began to arise out of the snow – a grand and powerful army. Their mangled bodies, now in spirit form, could be seen like a mighty rushing wind, gliding across the frozen landscape. All at once, thousands of Unknown Soldiers, still in the uniform they fought and died in, came and stood beside their General and saluted him.

Lt. Colonel Jameson asked, "What is happening Colonel, Sir?"

A mystified Colonel McDaniels replied, "I do not know. This must have been what the Angel was referring to."

Lt. Colonel Jameson shouted out, "Colonel, your uniform!" Somehow the Colonel McDaniels Union uniform was miraculously replaced with a General's uniform that was split down the middle. Union blue was on one side and Confederate gray on the other. Since time began, such a thing has never been seen before. Colonel McDaniels was indeed promoted in rank to

General of the Union and Confederate Unknown Soldiers. His incredible transformation was proof.

The Promise

Sitting cold and frozen in place, as Summer gradually opened her eyes, she could feel the snow on her injured hand and wondered what had just transpired. She could hear Katie's frantic voice in the foreground, and as her best friend almost reached her, Summer could feel herself being lifted up. It was the General standing Summer on to her feet. The General had not been that close to a woman in a very long time. But he knew she needed quick assistance or be forever lost in his world.

Her honeysuckle perfume filled the air, his mind and his senses. Other women had been on that hill before, yet he always looked away, as he tried to do with Summer. He fancied haunting the tourists as they came to town, especially the women. He was no gentleman! But the woman he held in his arms right now was different. The General knew what was revealed to her, as Summer saw history as it was taking place. When Katie reached her friend, she saw Summer's blood all around her on the snow. Because of her schooling in nursing, she knew Summer needed immediate help. Grabbing Summer by the shoulders, Katie asked, "Summer, listen to me! Are you able to climb down the hill with me?"

"Yes!" a dazed Summer responded. Knowing that there wasn't another person for miles, and she saw no other cars while she waited at the bottom of Big Round Top, Katie knew it was up to her to get her friend down this very steep and treacherous slope herself.

As the two began to trek back down Big Round Top, Summer suddenly stopped and glanced back over her right shoulder then said, "Thank you. I will be back and I promise I will do whatever I can to bring you peace."

It was the General who thought he had just seen, "a ghost!"

When Katie looked back to see who her friend was talking to, she saw no one and assumed her friend was disillusioned from shock. She knew it was critical at that moment to get Summer immediate medical attention. Worried for them both, Katie silently prayed for an Angel to help her. Little did she know, Angelic Beings had gathered all around that hill. The General was also holding onto Summer Ray. He too, knew it was critical to get her immediate medical attention, as she had just promised to do what she could to bring him and the Unknowns peace.

Once the girls reached the bottom and were safely inside the vehicle, a twinge of sadness filled the General. He could only trust in this frail little human - a human that was a woman no less! Could his pride stop him from believing in miracles?

As Katie drove the Blazer up and down through the Tops and Devil's Den, Summer Ray thought she saw a man walking toward Little Round Top. Still dazed and distracted from what just had happened on Big Round Top, Summer could not tell reality from fantasy. It was almost like a hallucination of some sort — like finding yourself in the desert, parched from lack of water and thinking you can see an oasis. The mind has the unfortunate ability to play tricks on humans when they most desperately need it to be still and truthful.

As the man walked beside the car, he stopped and looked at Summer Ray with the biggest and the most piercing blue eyes she had ever seen − eyes that punctured right through her soul. When he smiled at her, Summer put her hand up and touched the window as if to acknowledge his presence and speak. Words escaped her as this man literally took her breath away! As she looked back out the window at this stranger, Summer felt herself drifting in and out of consciousness, again!

On the way to the Gettysburg Hospital, Katie called Summer Ray's parents. By the time her parents made it to the hospital, Summer had lost a lot of blood and was in need of a transfusion. As she was walking out of the ladies restroom, she overheard Summer's dad tell the doctor something that rendered Kathryn Black speechless. Summer Ray Sherwood was adopted. It was the reason why neither of her parents' blood typed matched their daughter's. Katie stood frozen. She knew she would never be able to reveal such a secret as this and wished she had never heard it.

The Plan

Meanwhile, revolting dark and sinister spirits hovering over Big Round Top, without delay, reported all they saw and overheard to Woeburn. He was a fallen angel ruling over the town of Gettysburg. Woeburn was once a beautiful Angel named Aswell. His angelic bluish eyes turned demonic green and his heavenly wings were now broken behind his back. Beautiful hands that once played the "Harp of Heaven" were replaced with claws of a bear. His mouth that once worshipped the One True God, grew fangs of a serpent in imitation of his new god, the devil. Rancid foul odor spewed from his nostrils while he impatiently waited for a report from his subordinates at Devil's Den.

As the demons cowered before their prince, Dogwood, a small monkey looking creature with a long tail spoke up and said,

"There's little vermin of a woman who just promised to bring peace to the General and the Unknowns, my lord."

Woeburg demanded, "How can that be? They are forever tormented unable to rest. Only a human's blood that carries the Blood of the Lamb can..."

"What happened on that hill? Did her blood mix with theirs? Did she waken the Unknowns?" Woeburn questioned as his dark wings spanned open like the hood of a cobra.

Another wincing demon named Thacker, a gremlin with the face of a pig and hooves for hands, whimpered before his ruler and said, "'*The life of the flesh is in the blood;*' your most Wickedness and, like Abel, the voice of the soldiers' blood was crying '*up from the ground.*' When the creature fell, she cut her hand on a thorn bush and..."

The little imp was cut off by a sharp razor-like tail and was hurled off the rock, sniveling in pain.

Woeburn, their prince, ordered, "She must be stopped!"

Dogwood asked his master, "But how, your great Evilness? You know she carries the Blood of the Lamb. You know we cannot defeat the Blood."

111

Woeburn expressed with utmost satisfaction, "Yes! But we can weaken her to where she denies the Blood and renounces her faith." It gave the dark powers great delight to see a human soul dragged to Hell, especially one who once worshipped the Lamb. Their master, Satan, would grant any one of his workers more power if they brought to him the soul of Summer Ray and/or the souls of others like her, who may have once served the devil but had revolted against him.

Woeburn snorted with pleasure at the thought, and said, "We will make it seem like her God has abandoned her and thrown her away as if she were nothing more than rotten garbage. This Summer Ray won't remember her promise or Gettysburg for that matter. When we are finished with her, she won't remember the Enemy or His Blood."

All at once the Angels surrounding Gettysburg, now in a glorified state, began to assemble on the grounds of the Lutheran Seminary. Captain Talhelm was giving orders to the Heavenly Host as the SPIRIT was giving them to him. Summer Ray's Guardian Angel Rory, and a Warrior Angel named Sostar, were close at hand. It was their duty to protect Summer Ray.

Still, there are times when even Angels cannot interfere and must hold back until the SPIRIT allows them to intervene. Be that as it may, due to Sostar's zeal and his passion for war, there were times when other Angels had to reason with him to help him calm down. Even the Archangel Michael had to have a talk with his subordinate. Sostar would rather just slaughter all those foul demonic beings once and for all. But knowing that joy is for the Lord and the Lord alone, he patiently waits along with the rest of the innumerable company of Angels, and the human race who served the Lamb, for the glorious day when Satan and all his workers of iniquity would be cast finally into that deep dark abyss called "Hell."

As the dark and distorted creatures from the Underworld began to set up Summer's demise, the Light from above was not moved nor shaken by their malicious threats. If Summer Ray was truly theirs — the Father's, the Son's and the Holy Spirit's, no devil in Hell could bend her to the point of breaking her. Yet, that remained to be seen.

Ten years later...

CHAPTER FIVE

A Purpose

Summer Ray Sherwood, now divorced, was not the typical van-driving mom. Although she had the utmost respect for soccer moms, Summer just never fit the bill. Besides, she hated vans and wouldn't be caught dead owning one. A once promising figure skater, due to the injuries she sustained in a car accident, Summer was no longer able to compete. She turned her energy into becoming a Figure Skating Coach instead. So, after several years of working with her own Master Coach Elsabeth, Summer finally became a full-fledged certified coach herself.

The decision to become a coach was so successful and healing for Summer Ray that she decided to become a Special Olympics Figure Skating Coach as well. Whenever she would see one of her Special Olympics students attain a goal, they never thought they could, a humbled Summer would always break into tears. The car accident forced her into thinking of more than just herself. Perhaps that is why God allowed it to happen. The traps of self-absorption and self-pity are the worst. They are always self-inflicted traps. Coaching kept Summer on the ice and while helping others achieve their dreams, it gave Summer a sense of accomplishment and sparked her own flames of happiness. Summer knew that if she could overcome her own disabilities and continue ice skating, she could help others with disabilities to do the same.

Still, as a single mom, when things were financially hard on her, she would take her young son Billy across the street to King's Pizza. Lino would always give them free food and drinks. There are some friends you just cannot put a price tag on. Lino was definitely one of them. He was one of Summer Ray's angels.

Kathryn Black was Summer's best friend since elementary school. The dreams they had while growing up, had come true...sort of. They each married men they thought they loved. Summer was Kat's Matron of Honor at her wedding. Summer didn't have a wedding. She and Tommy just eloped. It was something she regretted the moment it happened. Her dream of a white gown and walking down the aisle was replaced with an emotionless corner room at the courthouse. There weren't any beautiful flowers displayed on the aisle of the church or the altar. There were no families or close friends in attendance to witness their nuptials. Just two strangers as witnesses who happened to be getting married right after their ceremony concluded. It was a mistake and they both knew it. When family and friends heard the news, they were crushed.

Summer's mom asked her daughter after she was already married, "Are you sure he's the one?"

It wasn't that she didn't like Tommy. Darlene, Summer's mom, just never saw the blending of souls between him and her daughter. When two people are really in love and are meant to be together, there is something almost magical about it. It just makes you happy to be around them. Summer's mom never once suspected that she was the *real* reason Summer Ray ran off. It was a secret Summer carried to her mother's death.

Though, for a while, life seemed to be good for Tom and Summer. Eventually though, the deterioration of their marriage began to materialize. Summer started

119

withdrawing from her friends, missed important meetings, canceled book signings and social events. As her marriage began to fall apart, the sparkle in her eyes for the life she so desperately was in love with began to dissipate as well. Despite her disabilities, Summer always found something to thank God for that inspired her to keep moving and to never give up.

Still, Tom never understood how damaging his affairs, his put downs and his demands affected her. He didn't love her through the "in sickness and in health" part, nor the "for better or for worse" part. He married Summer Ray without disabilities, and it was hard for Tom to adjust to a new kind of Summer. Summer stayed faithful to her husband through it all. But, even then, it just wasn't enough. That feeling of "just wasn't enough" tortured Summer. Then through the love and dedication of her God, her family and friends, she climbed out of the hole of self-pity and started a new life for her and her son.

Summer and Kat both wanted children and to raise their kids in the same area. Not wanting to see their friendship ripped apart because of distance, their families moved within three miles of each other. Billy - Summer's son, and Ella − Kat's daughter, were in the third grade together and attend Madison Elementary School in Frederick, Maryland. After Summer's accident, due to her severe head injury, at times her speech was affected, too. Summer had a hard time saying her best friend's name. So "Katie" became "Kat". It was easier for Summer and Kat graciously obliged.

Traumatic Brain Injury

It was Wednesday evening at the Sherwood house. Summer just finished coaching at the ice rink and was determined to make a home cooked meal. Kat walked into the kitchen and asked, "What are you cooking for dinner?"

Summer defensively replied, "I haven't figured that out yet."

Her friend politely questioned, "Want me to help?"

Summer, trying her best to hold back tears, defiantly responded, "No Kat. I keep trying to tell you that, over and over again. I don't want your help, or anybody else's for that matter. I have to do this myself."

Kat firmly told her friend, "Do what yourself? The kids and I are starving and you have been staring at that cookbook for over fifteen minutes."

Summer shot back at her friend, "That isn't nice."

Kat lovingly but firmly responded, "It isn't meant to be nice, Summer Ray. It is reality, and a reality that you need to start getting a grip on. This obsession of yours is nothing more than your stupid pride. You have to get over it and accept there are certain things you just cannot do anymore."

Summer kept up with her defense, as she slammed shut the cookbook, "You just don't understand. I have to do this."

Kat, now standing in front of a crying Summer, through her own tears said, "Do what Summer? What is it that you HAVE to do? Tell me so I will understand

122

and leave you alone about it. What exactly are you trying to prove here?"

Summer, close to sobbing, uttered the best she could, "You dooon't understand, Kat. I keep tryyying to tell you that and you are not listening to me. Nobody is listening to me. I am not trying to prove anything. I just want to be normal."

Kathryn Black, in a very serious, concerned tone, said back to her best friend, "Define normal. Before your accident 'normal', or living with Traumatic Brain Injury 'normal'? You know you cannot go back to the 'normal' you knew before your accident, Summer Ray. That part of your life is over and the sooner you wake up to that fact, the better off you and Billy will be. You keep telling me, I don't understand. You are right, I don't. I can't. But I love you and I love Billy. I see what you are doing to both you and him, and it is tearing me apart to have to watch it. How many times last week did you almost burn the house down because you forgot there was food cooking on the stove?

We have been best friends since the 2nd grade. I was there when they brought you to Shock Trauma half dead. I saw you broken, bruised and barely breathing. Whether you believe it or not Summer Ray, I shared that accident with you. I was there every day, waiting for you to come out of your coma. When Tommy had to work or stay home to take care of Billy, I stayed with you through the night and held your hand. I didn't let go. I couldn't bear to lose my best friend. When they finally released you from the hospital, do you remember how determined you were to skate again? It was all you thought about. I was there when you took your first baby steps out on that ice. I couldn't have been prouder. But, this? This Summer Ray is different. If you burn the house down, you and Billy could die. Is that what you want all for the sake of being normal?"

Summer exclaimed, "They said I couldn't skate again. Look at me. I am skating."

A now sad Kat had to inform her disillusioned friend, "Yes! It is true you are skating. But, Summer Ray, that is all you are doing. You are not competing, or jumping are you? Do you think this is easy for me to have stand here and say these things to you? It is breaking my heart. But if you do not start accepting the cards that have

124

been dealt to you, instead of ignoring them, you and Billy could both die!"

It appeared that reality was starting to finally sink in, as Summer put her head down with her face in her hands. When she finally was able to look up at Katie she asked, "What do I do Kat? Tell me! You know I don't want to hurt Billy."

Kat put her hands lovingly on Summer's shoulders and told her, "You call your sponsor at the brain injury clinic and get yourself into that Traumatic Brain Injury support group. They can help you where I can't. They understand what I do not. They will teach you how to function on a daily basis without the threat of you harming yourself, your son or anyone else for that matter."

A frustrated Summer said, "I am not ready for that. You know that, Kat. So please, stop hounding me about it." When Billy saw his momma walk over to pick up her cell phone, with his elbow he jabbed Ella, and with a big smile he said, "I told you it was pizza night."

After Summer hung up the phone, she called for her son. "Billy, I need to see your book bag, please."

"Nice way to change the subject, Summer Ray," a discouraged Kat griped. Yet, when an excited Billy took out the notice about the field trip to Gettysburg, an old familiar sense washed over Summer.

A bubbly, brown haired, light green-eyed Billy asked his momma, "Mom, can you chaperone?"

Smiling at her son, Summer asked him, "Do I have to?"

An anxious Billy replied, "I have to bring the paper back tomorrow. So, make sure you sign it, Mom."

Kat asked her friend, "So, what is going through that stubborn and thick head of yours, Ms. Summer Ray Sherwood?"

"You're going!" Summer informed her best friend.

Kat jokingly responded, "Seeing you chaperone five, loud, boisterous third graders, I wouldn't miss it for the world."

Upon seeing Summer flash her one of those looks, Kat answered back, "I know, Summer. I know. I will make arrangements to put Ella in your group so I can help you." Then Kat laughingly said, "Trust me. I won't throw you to the wolves."

Due to her previous car accident, Summer Ray suffered from Traumatic Brain Injury. Though still in self-denial at times, she learned how to manage her memory loss; her lack of ability to make choices at a department store and her loss of feeling in almost half her body. Billy got used to his Aunt Katie's home cooking and his mom's frozen dinners. When Billy was with his dad, Tommy made sure Billy had four or five course meals. Sometimes Summer thought Tommy only did that to make her feel worse about herself. But even if he did, Summer knew Tom gave their son at least some sense of normalcy at the dinner table.

Still, Summer, on occasions, had Kat and Ella over to make cookies with her and Billy. Of course, they were the pre-measured, pre-made, all ready to go, just pop them in the oven kind of cookies. Kat was just there to supervise the oven – most of the time, or when Summer would let her that is. Yet, other times when Summer was in one of her "I have to prove to the world that I can cook" moods, Kat tried the best she could to not interfere.

Summer depended on Kathryn Black as if she were a crutch and/or her own personal assistant. Although Summer wished she wasn't dependent, she couldn't go back in time to erase that other car that slammed into her car head on. It was raining and the other car lost control and crossed the center line. Luckily no one was killed. Summer Ray was alone in her car and though critically injured her life and the life of the other driver was spared. Thank God for air bags and Angels, as Summer Ray would have been dead without them.

Due to the force of impact, Summer's brain jolted back and forth inside her skull. Thankfully, only the back part of her brain suffered damage. Had the front been damaged as well, Summer would have died for sure. So, how do you live your life in self-pity, knowing how close you came to not having a life at all? Summer knew God spared her life. She knew He protected her from death.

Still, she felt like her life at times had become a living hell. The excruciating pain almost caused her to

128

commit suicide. But, one look at that beautiful little boy of hers, Summer Ray knew she had to endure. She had many fights with God, or rather she lashed out and He patiently listened. When the doctors diagnosed her with TBI, they said her "fits of rage" were normal. Soon after, due to the pain level, they put her on narcotic pain medication. It wasn't long before Summer Ray became medically dependent, then totally addicted.

Her coach Elsabeth, also a pastor, never once judged her for her addiction. She would simply take her off the ice and tell her she loved her. You simply cannot skate high or drunk. If you cannot stand up or walk a straight line on dry pavement, you certainly cannot do either on ice. When the sad realization hit Summer Ray that she just couldn't compete like she used to, it was almost as if she felt the devil was laughing at her and that he felt he had won somehow. Well, that was all she wrote. From that moment on, Summer resolved she would skate, even if it was only to teach others and to help them achieve their dreams.

Summer Ray was not one to be thrown under the bus by anyone, especially the devil. Her new-found inspiration to become a coach delighted Elsabeth. It was an idea she had many times thought herself, but one she knew Summer would have to decide on her own. Sometimes the hardest part of change is accepting that change isn't an option. Summer then, at her own church, stood up before everyone and finally admitted that she was a drug addict. The weight of lying was lifted off her shoulders as no longer did she have to pretend. What she could hide from others, she could not hide from herself. When Summer pulled out the pills from her pocket, the congregation gasped. Summer knew the only way to deliverance was through God and the truth. Miraculously, through confession, prayer and the power of God, Summer was almost instantly free of her addiction.

When Summer finally accepted the reality of her loss from that accident, she gained a purpose. When she lost the heart of her husband Tommy, she gained another purpose. Behind every loss is a purpose just waiting to be birthed. It had become Summer Ray Sherwood's mission to make sure of it, at least in her own life.

CHAPTER SIX

The Field Trip

Gettysburg was a forty-minute bus ride from Billy's elementary school. Summer, a chaperone on her son's field trip, was able to take time off work to spend the day with him. When Billy's dad offered to go on the field trip with them, Summer told him, "No!"

Though godly, Summer would rather have offered a rather large, "Hell No!" instead, but with Billy listening intently while his mom was on the phone with his dad, she kept her composure. Billy's dad wasn't the best dad. But she had to admit he wasn't the worst either. He led a life of hard work, video games and loose women. It was the latter two which led to the ruin of their marriage, but in his own real way he did love his son. Still, Summer did not want this trip to Gettysburg to be full of tension between her and Billy's dad. She almost lied when she told him, "They did not need another chaperone." It was sort of true. They didn't need another chaperone. But what she failed tell him was that the school allowed for parents as extras, if they wanted to go. Summer grinned and thought to herself, "No! He didn't need to get THAT memo."

Besides, it was Gettysburg. For whatever reason, yet unknown to her, Gettysburg held the key to her past, present and future. Oftentimes Summer would have the strangest yet the most beautiful of all visions. She saw her own spirit gliding down the streets of Gettysburg and at times hovering near one of the shops. How do you describe your own spirit without sounding conceited? The visions of Summer's spirit were truly the most beautiful she had ever seen. She was outlined in white, with long flowing white hair and wearing a long white gown. On her head it looked like she was wearing a crown made of flowers and baby's breath.

She was always smiling in these visions. The splendor of these visions was the presence of Light that surrounded her. You could tell it was heavenly. But how was it possible to be a spirit in Gettysburg, while your body and soul were living in Maryland? It was like being in two places at the same time. Maybe it was why she felt at home in Gettysburg. She was in her element. Some things Summer Ray just could not explain.

Had this field trip been to Kings Dominion or Hershey Park, the responsible thing for her to have done would have been to let Tommy chaperone. Since her brain injury, Summer no longer found amusement parks so amusing.

Summer and Kat had five kids in their group including their own. Not only was her best friend there to help Summer Ray chaperone, it was planned this way so that Summer could venture off at lunch time to visit The Evergreen Cemetery where Mary Virginia Wade, or Jennie Wade for short was buried. Her real nick name is "Ginny" not "Jennie." Unfortunately, down through the ages of history past, Ginny became Jennie.

Kat knew of Summer's passion for Gettysburg. But like everyone else who questioned it, she didn't understand what Summer was so passionate about. Summer didn't even know. She only knew it was important for her to find out. Without a car on this field trip, parents and students had to walk, walk and walk.

The actual bus tour around Gettysburg didn't start until 12:30PM. So that meant an 11:30AM lunch.

It was a typical June day with temperatures climbing to the high 80's. Only a half hour into the tour, some of the kids and chaperones had already started complaining of the walking and the heat. Summer didn't mind the walk. She minded the gnawing in her stomach that something just wasn't right. It was as if something or someone was out of place. As an historian, Summer understood the Civil War. But, that stupid accident that almost cost her - her life, cost much of her memory. She constantly had to re-learn the history she so dearly loved. Summer read about the Gettysburg ghosts and never gave them much mind. "Just stories," she told herself.

Besides, she was still a very strong Christian woman and ghosts in her opinion just did not exist. She was too worried she would end up following some demon, not a real ghost of a Civil War soldier or one of those orphans she read so much about. So, she closed her mind to it all and just forced herself not to think about it.

While she was on this field trip in Gettysburg, the one thing she was determined to do was to visit The Evergreen Cemetery and not just because of Jennie Wade. This cemetery is where President Abraham Lincoln gave his famous "Gettysburg Address" speech, on November 19, 1863 and is located next to The Gettysburg National Cemetery. So, as Summer and Kat's group was settling in for lunch, Summer let her know she would be just across the street.

Her friend just smiled and said, "Sure! Take your time. Hey and don't forget to come back. You are not leaving me alone with all these kids." Summer grinned as she replied, "Now, would I do that?"

Summer hugged her son, Billy and told him, "I will be just across the street. Please keep an eye on your Aunt Katie. I will be right back." As hungry and as thirsty as he was, Billy didn't mind that mom checked out of the group, just that he could cool off. He knew his Aunt Katie would make sure he would eat and drink. He trusted his momma was close by and would return as fast as she left.

Side-By-Side

Jennie Wade was the only civilian to die in the Civil War battle at Gettysburg. Summer read her story over and over again, and always with the same sadness at the tragic ending. Summer constantly wished she could somehow re-write history and give Jennie and Jack the happy ending they deserved instead. Jennie and Jack didn't fail each other, the war failed them. Though dying for one's country is perhaps one of the greatest of all sacrifices, it still did not make it right for Jennie and Jack to not be buried side-by-side. Even if no one else carried her same conviction, that is how Summer believed it should be.

In fact, the Civil War was despised by the hopeless romantic in Summer. Why the South wanted to secede from the North never truly made sense to her. But, hopeless romantics and historians, like Summer Ray, are always trying to re-write the parts of history that are permanently etched on the pages of time past. Though her memory needed to be refreshed due to her accident, Gettysburg remained close to her heart. Summer knew slavery was wrong. She also knew that a war of this brutality and horrific means did not have to happen to see the slaves freed. After all, the Civil War didn't start due to slavery, at least not from a Northern point of view.

It was however a Southern point of view as the South needed the slaves for its economic purposes. Freeing the slaves was used as a strategic means of weakening the Confederate economy. The Emancipation Proclamation signed by President Abraham Lincoln on January 1, 1863 did just that. It is however, a proven fact that many of those freed slaves joined the Confederacy to fight against the Union. In the midst of such dark and trying circumstances, no one can fully comprehend why any human being during that time period acted the way they did.

Yet with all of President Abraham Lincoln's efforts to save the Union, none of those gallant efforts could stop tragedy from happening to Jennie and Jack. Jennie Wade was in love with a United States soldier named Corporal Jack Skelly. They were childhood friends growing into blossoming sweethearts. Jennie loved her Jack. Summer often compared her shallow love for Tom, to that of Jennie's deep love to Jack. "Not even close," she thought.

In itself, that should have been a warning flag. Summer was desperate to keep up with the rest of her friends, who at the time were getting married before they were thirty. Summer wanted nothing more than to escape the doldrums of her controlling mother who tried to keep her involved in witchcraft. Tommy and Summer met at college and shared the ice as a common bond. He was a goal-tender for Mt. Saint Mary's College. Summer and Tommy married on a whim and divorced in disaster. Though the malice of war broke out around Jack and Jennie, their hearts were joined together by the sweet encompassing love of the universe. Between the two of them, though short lived, they shared the entrenching gift of true love that so few are lucky to ever find. The only thing divine from Summer's marriage to Tommy was Billy. Summer Ray would forever be thankful for her Billy.

Jennie Wade was buried three different times before she was interred in The Evergreen Cemetery. The cemetery used to be a favorite retreat for Jennie − a quiet place to sit and read and pray. Before their dreadful and untimely deaths, Jack and Jennie met there, exchanging vows of love to each other. Strange isn't it? One of the last times they saw each other was in a cemetery. Had that been a sign of their impending doom or was it more of a sign of their eternal love? Shortly after the war, Jack Skelly was also interred at The Evergreen Cemetery. Now, in that same cemetery, Jack and Jennie are together again, though not buried side-by-side.

Jack was mortally wounded in Winchester, Virginia and asked their mutual childhood friend Wesley Culp, to give a message to Jennie that he was dying. Wesley Culp who also grew up in Gettysburg, to keep his job building carriages, traveled to Shepherdstown, Virginia when the business moved. While employed in Virginia, the Civil War broke out and Wesley felt it was his duty to join The Army of Northern Virginia − the Confederates. Wesley was deemed a traitor in Gettysburg and if found by the Unions, he would have faced public humiliation and possible torture. When he found Jack at a Confederate hospital, Jack asked him to deliver a message to Jennie:

"He had loved her and that he was sorry he could not be returning to Gettysburg."

Some ghost people believe had Wesley lived to give the message, he would not have. They claimed he too was in love with Jennie. Still other ghost people believed, "He would never do such a thing."

The only problem with history is that no one actually knows the whole truth or the real truth. Modern day historians can only try the best they can to calculate truth based on the information left behind. However, it seems the Bible, down through the ages of time past, *is* the only thing that *holds* the whole and real truth. Still, the devil has done a good job of trying to counterfeit even the "Good Book" by other means. Yet, the Bible can no man or devil imitate as it is the living, breathing Word of God.

Fate was cruel to Jennie, Jack and Wesley! Jennie was killed on July 3rd, 1863 around 8:30AM by a stray bullet from a Confederate sharpshooter, shooting from a window at the Farnsworth House. Though it doesn't seem logistically possible, that is how history was written.

Wesley Culp died an hour or two before Jennie did. He was shot to death, adjacent to his uncle's farm and never did get to give Jennie the message from Jack. Wesley's body was never found and to this day, no one really knows where he is buried. Jack died a long agonizing nine days after Jennie and Wesley, in a Confederate hospital. No one knew Jennie Wade would never see the face of her beloved, Jack Skelly, ever again nor that he would never see hers.

After she was killed, Jennie's mother searched Jennie's dress pockets and found a picture of Jack. Back in the Civil War era, only women who were either betrothed or already married carried pictures of their men in their dresses. It just was not suitable behavior or proper etiquette in those days for a woman who wasn't married or betrothed to carry men's pictures in their pockets. It just wasn't! So, was it possible then and is it possible now, to be married to someone in your heart, even if there isn't the legal paperwork to back it up? Jennie's mother did not like Jack Skelly at all. But, upon seeing the picture of him that Jennie carried inside her dress pocket, one can only imagine the amount of regret

Jennie's mother felt for hating him so much. Her daughter loved him and that should have been enough.

At least theirs was a "real love." Summer thought. But still it did not shake the feeling she had in the pit of her stomach that something just wasn't right about it. It didn't take long for Summer to find Jennie Wade's grave. All she had to do was to look for the American flag standing tall and proud by her gravesite. Upon hearing the news of Jennie's death, due to her kneading dough to make biscuits or bread for the Union soldiers, President Lincoln had an American flag placed by her gravesite. It was ordered to never fly at half-staff and to this day, it never has. She was given full honors for her sacrifice. The same honor was given to only one other woman in history and that was Betsy Ross.

When Summer stopped to look at Jennie's grave, she wondered in which direction she could find Jack Skelly. She heard Jack's grave was only seventy-five paces from Jennie's. So up and down gravesites she walked in every direction, but still she could not find him. As soon as a frustrated Summer began to walk back to her group from the field trip, a man in the distance, without speaking a word, commanded her attention.

A Ghost

The Unknowns were not sure if the General was just being a gracious ghost that day, or if this woman in particular caught his eye for another reason. Only the General could become visible in human form anywhere in Gettysburg, except The Gettysburg National Cemetery that is. The Unknowns could only become visible in human form on Big Round Top. When the General was mortally wounded at the Wheat Field, he was still recognizable as well as his Lt. Colonel George Jameson. The Colonel was later interred, in what was called, the Soldiers National Cemetery with a stone that read:

Colonel Michael Moses McDaniels
Army of the Potomac
Killed July 2, 1863
WHEAT FIELD; GETTYSBURG, PA

143

Because the General felt the death of his men was entirely his fault, he chose to stay with them sacrificing his own peace, in order to bring them theirs.

When Summer noticed him across the cemetery, one of those peculiar feelings swept over her. She was certain she had never seen him before. But due to her memory loss, Summer could not trust her own intuition. The General was wearing a faded black shirt and faded blue jeans. He had striking black and graying hair and wow, was he ever gorgeous. While he was looking at her, he was also pointing his finger down at what appeared to be a gravesite. Lost in thought, when Summer looked back at the man he was gone. She knew she had only looked away from him for a few seconds and there was nowhere for him to go, at least not that fast.

Despite the fact that what just happened was really creepy, Summer did not have time to analyze it. But she was curious as to what her handsome stranger was pointing at. So, she walked and counted her steps in what WAS his direction. When she walked seventy-five paces, she looked down and sure enough, it was Jack

144

Skelly's grave. Summer then said out loud, "Okay! This is really REALLY weird."

She didn't see the General just a few feet away from her laughing at her, as he turned back into spirit form. The General loved to play tricks on the tourists. Remember, he was no gentleman! But when he caught a glimpse of her face up close and when a familiar honeysuckle perfume began to fill the air, one that he could never forget, the General's attention was abruptly fixated on Summer. He began questioning this woman's face, her hair, her smell and her eyes, yeah especially her eyes. Could this be the scrawny young woman he had seen on the Tops years before? Is she the one who promised to come back and never did? Had he seen her before?

Although he knew millions of tourists over the years had been to Gettysburg, he never remembered any of them, just the regulars. But this woman had intrigued him. He saw Summer look around for him and when she began to walk away from Jack's grave toward the exit of the cemetery on Baltimore Street, he followed her. Although she thought "tall, dark and handsome" was

145

only for Hollywood movies, this man definitely fit the description. He was definitely tall, tanned and oh so handsome! He was muscular and mysterious.

"Yeah like that wasn't hard to notice!" Summer blushed.

Yet as strong as he looked physically, the look in his dark brown eyes was that of longing. Even across the cemetery she could see it. It was almost as if she saw it before. It was as if he was hurting somehow and Summer could feel his pain. When she composed herself enough to look at him again, he was gone. Had she just seen a ghost? How could a ghost have such depth in his eyes? Summer didn't even know what to call it or him.

"Okay!" Summer said to herself, "Get a grip." Yes, he was handsome. So handsome in fact that she almost knocked over a vending table on her way back to the group because she was in such a state of shock at seeing whoever or whatever it was she just saw. Luckily Billy saw her and ran up to his mother.

"A distraction," she thought.

Summer asked her son, "Billy, are you having fun?"

Billy replied, "Yeah, but I want to see the cannons, please Mom." Kat noticed the baffled and perplexed looked in Summer's expression and said, "Wow Summer! You look like you have just seen a ghost! What is it?"

When the General heard the name "Summer," he was almost outraged. He then asked the Lt. Colonel by his side, "Is this the Summer Ray who promised me she would be back?"

The Lt. Colonel only replied, "I do not know, General, Sir."

Summer expressed to her son, "Billy, you know you are not supposed to grab Mommy's hand that hard."

A sorrowful Billy replied, "Oh yeah, I forgot. Sorry, Mom." Summer urged him, "Please try to remember, Son."

An exasperated Billy shrugged his shoulders and said, "Okay, Mom, okay!"

By this time, the General had followed Summer Ray to Cemetery Hill. When Summer turned her right hand over to rub the pain out of her palm, the General invisibly stood by her and held her hand to look at it. He saw the scars from when she had grabbed onto the thorn bush at Big Round Top. Although Summer felt something tugging at her hand, she couldn't see what that something was. When she tried to pull her hand back from whatever it was that held it, she had to use her other hand to try to jerk her arm back. But the General quickly shoved down her hand, practically knocking Summer over, and then left in disgust.

An anxious Billy asked his mom, "Can we go see the cannons? They are just right over there?"

An assertive Kat told the group, "Okay kids, finish up. We have to get ready for the bus tour."

Summer asked Kat, "Billy wants to see the cannons. Do we have a few minutes? We can take some cute pictures there."

Kat quietly questioned her friend, "Summer, what is going on? You look nervous and your voice is crackling. What the hell happened over there at that cemetery, or do I really want to know?"

Summer assured her friend, "It's nothing Kat."

"It's always nothing," Kat said and continued, "Why am I not surprised? Okay kids let's head to those

148

cannons for some quick pictures," she said to the excited and rambunctious group. Things were getting a little too bizarre for Summer. She was glad the field trip was almost over and just the bus tour was left.

Summer silently prayed, "Oh God, please let it be quiet!"

CHAPTER SEVEN

Embittered

Back on Big Round Top, the General was pacing back and forth hollering, "She forgot her promise! How could she forget? She's a traitor just like my ex-wife." When the General was angry, it was best to let him be. Some of the Unknowns had made the mistake of trying to pacify the General in a fit of rage and found themselves flown half way across Gettysburg. The General was known to fight first and talk later. He wasn't a controlled officer, at least not since the war.

The General wasn't an Unknown Soldier. He was a Colonel who chose to stay behind to help his men and others like them cross over to the other side. It was for this reason he became the General and why he was able to become visible to humans as Angels and demons can. The General never forgave himself for the loss of his men. He blamed their slaughter on a weak moment while thinking of his newly ex-wife Lily, and not on the battle at hand. Perhaps it was the timing of the letter he received from the courier on the second day of battle, July 2, 1863. It was shocking to receive such shocking news, while fighting for the Union at one of the most gruesome battles on American soil. But the Colonel was still an American soldier. He would never put his heart before his country. Still, unbeknown to him, there was nothing he could do to prevent their deaths nor his own, had he not stopped to think of his ex–wife.

When Ariel, the glorious Angel of Welcome came to escort him into Heaven, Michael Moses McDaniels refused. To this day, only the gatekeepers passed down from generation to generation, know of the Unknowns existence in Gettysburg. The only one who was granted contact to the General and the Unknowns in present day, was Summer Ray and that was when she slipped and sliced open her hand on Big Round Top years before. Sadly, she could remember neither the battle she saw, nor the promise she had made.

The General's Pride

The General McDaniels did not forget. In fact, it infuriated him that he thought she had lied to him. The General had lost all faith in humanity, especially in women. He knew most women were romantics, though most women did not include his ex-wife. She, who promised to wait for him for forever, did not even wait two years. If the General could just forgive himself and forgive his ex-wife, his heart would no longer be bitter. It was precisely what Ariel warned him against. With a bitter heart, he could not find the peace he so desperately needed and the peace his men and others like them also needed.

Summer, in his opinion, was just as much of a traitor as his ex-wife as she did not keep her promise either. It was not so much a promise to the General that concerned him. It was a promise of peace to his soldiers that he was obsessed with. Without the Unknowns being free from their torment, the General knew he would be forever stuck in his. He knew the Unknowns needed the chance for peace and eternal rest to be given to them. If they chose to accept it, that was their choice. But the occasion still needed to present itself. Little did the General know, the opportunity already presented itself, thousands of times before. But, the Unknowns were not any different than other soldiers serving under the Stars and Stripes. They too, were fiercely loyal to their commanding officer and simply refused to abandon him.

For the General to find peace and eternal rest, it was as simple as clicking his heels. Like Dorothy in Oz, who only had to click her heels three times to get back to Kansas. Yet, it took traveling the yellow brick road for her to finally understand what home really meant to her and for her to ever be able to return to it. For the General to return to his home, his real home in Heaven, he still had to defeat his own demons – the demon of unforgiveness and the demon of bitterness. Both will keep any human soul out of Heaven for sure and for all eternity.

Such a tragedy when all one has to do is forgive. Love cannot grow in a heart full of poison. Poison kills where love heals. The world surely does not need mankind spreading more poison around. Is that not what the devil does? Is that not his job to be full of evil and hate? Why then does the human heart allow itself to become what he is and to do what he does? Doesn't he steal, kill and destroy enough? Humans certainly do not need to help him. Though he enjoys the assistance of humans who follow on his path to death and devastation, he certainly does not need a human to support it. He does enough destruction on his own.

CHAPTER EIGHT

Her Faith

Although Gettysburg might not be Kansas, there were sure enough witches, lions, tigers and bears on the loose. None of which would do Summer Ray any good, if she had to withstand any of them. It was true, however, because of her many years of struggle due to immense physical suffering and loss of self-esteem, Summer had developed strength and confidence in God. Yet, the devil knew her weakness. It was her hopeless romanticism and belief in happy endings that at times, made Summer choose unwisely and fall prey to the devil's schemes. Though her car accident almost killed her, it was the betrayal of her husband that damaged her the most.

Summer, though not passionately in love with Tom at the time of their divorce, was more crushed because she didn't want Billy, to have to suffer the consequences of their mistakes. Her dream of marriage and family was blown to bits and the reality of it broke her heart and crushed her soul. Stephen Berry in his book, "*House of Abraham – Lincoln & The Todds, A Family Divided By War*"[2] wrote the following:

Elijah Babbit warned his fellow Americans in the 1860's:

'*Feuds which exist between members of the same families, where they do exist, are the most bitter of all feuds. Wars (between) the same people...are the most bloody, the most savage, and the longest continued, of any wars that take place in the world.*'

Mary Chestnut penned in her famous diary:

'*We are divorced, North from South, because we hated each other so.*'

Summer Ray would soon face the darkest battle she ever had to fight. The fight to keep her faith in the God she loved. But war, divorce, disappointment, pain, suffering, heartache and abandonment has ways of leaving their marks on one's core. How much can the human soul stand before it begins to falter in its trust in the God that allows such brutality? Ultimately, God decides what the devil is allowed to do and what he isn't allowed to do. If all these trials and tribulations are nothing more than to test one's faith, is it possible that even God Himself could go too far? Although Summer would never kneel or bow to the devil she hated, was it possible for her to stop kneeling and to stop bowing to the God she loved?

Ability to Choose

Summer hated the devil with a passion. She grew up in witchcraft and finally got free from it when she got saved at seventeen. Yet in order to survive and defeat a devil that pursued her, if she wanted to stay alive, she had no choice but to learn about Spiritual Warfare. It wasn't an enjoyable thing to have to learn, however every

Christian needed some understanding of warfare and a solid foundation in knowing who they were in Christ.

Although Summer suffered a great deal of trials and tribulations over the past thirteen years, she never once turned back to witchcraft. The temptation to cast a spell on someone, to read someone's future with Tarot Cards, to look into the spirit world using crystals, or to converse with the spirit world at a séance, always tried to rear its ugly head. But like a rattlesnake about to strike, the only way to keep Summer Ray and her family from harm was to cut off temptation's ugly head using the power of the Word of God. She knew that just beyond the temptation was tragic sin. Besides, Summer was fervently in love with God and all He stood for. No one could take her from Him. Still, God always gave her a choice. She could turn back to witchcraft if she wanted to. It is the beauty of God. He never forces His will on anyone. He gave mankind the incredible ability to choose. It is called, "*free will.*"

Though countless humans try to blame the devil for their actions, he simply does not have that kind of power, unless of course, a human willingly gives himself

160

or herself over to him. In that case, he graciously will oblige. When that one drink turned into thousands, when that addiction finally took hold, it was still the choice of the alcoholic to take that first drink. It started out simple enough. But the devil forgot to inform the alcoholic, the drug addict, or the food addict, that the results of their addiction was directly related to their own lack of self-control.

But it was *his* goal, to get them addicted. Does not addiction steal, kill and destroy? The Bible says in John 10:10, "*The thief does not come except to steal, and to kill and to destroy.*" So, the devil got what he wanted and he wasn't even trying. The addict and the alcoholic are left in utter despair, wondering how their lives became so impossible and out of control.

Betrayal

Summer was twenty-three years old when she was critically injured in a car accident. Due to her injuries, Summer had little memory of her childhood or much of her life prior to the crash. The amnesia, the disabilities, the struggles and the long hours of physical therapy, were all things her husband Tommy could not deal with. The answer to his unhappiness was other women. When Summer found out her husband was cheating on her, what felt like a million knives had impaled her heart. The only words he said were, "I have just started seeing her, get over it!"

Betrayal is never easy at any age, regardless if he was the man of her dreams or not. Summer still loved him. Yet, he was vicious, careless and heartless. Summer never thought she would heal from such a devastating wound. Even the trauma she suffered from her accident, was still nowhere near as painful as the heartache caused by her husband.

However, it was true what Thomas Paine in 1794 once stated:

> "*All grief, like all things else, will yield to the obliterating power of time.*"[3]

The problem with so many people is that they can only see the grief and choose to commit suicide instead. It has been said that one should not just try to hold on but reach for a better tomorrow. Summer never understood that logic. If someone is at the end of their rope, the only thing left to do is to tie a knot and hang on. They can only hold on until they are rescued. It has also been said, "God only helps those who help themselves."

The was more logic Summer never understood. If that were true, no one on planet Earth would survive. Sometimes all people *can* do is hold on and nothing else. So, does God just let them sit there to dangle? Or does He wait for a lost soul to cry out to Him? Summer knew she had responsibilities. She knew she had to climb out of her hole of self-pity. It was her choice to do so. It was God's grace that catapulted her to be able to do so.

Time did eventually heal the heartache. Summer had to admit to herself that she and Billy were much better off without her ex-husband, or without them living together as a family. Billy was no longer subjected to his mother's tears and his father's irresponsible behavior. He was careless and Summer

163

finally found a place of serenity. She didn't want her son raised in that kind of environment. Summer knew God would provide a better man. She just had to have patience. It was something she knew she was greatly lacking. She did, however, have the courage to say, "No!" to the wrong things and to the wrong men.

Same Old Sinking Feeling

Summer still believed that dreams could come true. She never gave up hope of finding the man that she was perfect for. Quite often, Summer would find herself dreaming of a man handing her a pocket watch. But not being able to remember more of the details almost haunted her. Other times she would wake up bewailing. All she could see in these dreams were rocks, blood, smoke and her running after something or someone in what appeared to be in desperation.

She hated her memory loss. It almost felt at times as if she wasn't real and as if nothing else was real either.

Time would stop and then it would start all over again, leaving missing pieces behind. Although she hated being alone without a man in her life, she wasn't about to make the same mistake with regards to men. She knew waiting on God was the only option. It was the only path to walk and she knew it. Never mind the times when she would secretly cry herself to sleep. Sometimes she even felt let down and misunderstood by the God she loved more than anything. Men had asked Summer out on several occasions, only to be given the same response of, "No! Thank you!"

Summer at other times felt like there was something wrong with her. She just couldn't bring herself to say, "Yes!" to any of the men who had asked her out, without having that *same old sinking feeling* in her stomach. In the words of Arthur Martine in his book "*Handbook of Etiquette,*"[4]

> "*Every young woman ought to know the state of her own heart.*"

165

Summer knew the state of her own heart alright and she knew she would have to wait for the man who took that sinking feeling away. When she saw the man in her dreams, gripping her with those eyes, that sinking feeling went away, but then again, so did the man! Life seemed to be playing a cruel joke on Summer Ray. As an author, Summer always searched for answers. But it was getting to where she didn't know the right questions to ask anymore. When questions were asked of her, she also knew she could no longer answer them. It was like not knowing who you were. It was a horrible feeling, even with God's Word in her heart.

Summer called her son from her office and asked, "Can you please let Max out and get ready for bed?"

Billy asked his worn-out mom, "Can't I stay up and watch more T.V.? Huh, Mom?"

An exhausted Summer told her son, "Billy, it's late. You have your camping trip with your dad in the morning."

Billy, trying to reason with his momma said, "Yeah, Mom that is why I have to stay up. I can't sleep."

Summer sounded almost irritated, "Just take Max out please and go to bed. I will be up soon to check on you."

God Gives Grace to the Humble

Due to her accident, when Summer felt overwhelmed, she would just shut down. Billy could see his momma shutting down and decided not to rock the boat. He knew the results were never good in his favor if he pushed her too far and he really wanted to go camping. Billy gave in and as he hugged his mom he told her, "Okay! I am going to bed. I love you, Mom."

Billy called for Max as he opened the sliding glass door. A few minutes later, after letting the dog in, Billy could be heard yelling out to Summer, "Okay, Mom, Max is in."

Summer replied, "Thanks, Son. I will be up in a few."

Billy went upstairs with Luke, his Guardian Angel, following close behind. Once in his room, he

167

crawled underneath his Pittsburgh Penguins quilt. Though he lived in Caps country close to Washington D.C. the Penguins were Billy's favorite professional ice hockey team. The New York Rangers were Summer's favorite team and the Washington Caps were her dad's. When the Rangers and the Penguins played against each other, sparks usually flew around the Sherwood house, as mom and son shouted for opposing teams.

Billy loved to play ice hockey. As soon as he was able to walk, Summer Ray put ice skates on her little boy. His room was filled with ice hockey posters, figurines and an autographed picture of the Penguins. His first pair of ice skates and hockey stick were on display downstairs in the living room. They were hung over the fireplace for family and friends to see. Summer could not be prouder of her son. Billy was only a year old when Summer had her accident. Though barely able to walk herself, Summer Ray was determined not to let her newly found disabilities stop her from being a good mom. Her son could very well have been the *real* reason Summer Ray was able to stay focused and why she refused to allow herself to remain in a sea of sorrow and self-pity.

Summer turned the light off in her office, shut the door and went to the kitchen to check the stove. She said out loud as she looked at the burners, "Off, off, off, off. No red lights on. Off, off, off, off." She then turned to leave the kitchen, walked back to the stove and repeated this process at least four more times. Part of Summer's injury left her with Obsessive Compulsive Disorder, or OCD for short. This nightly routine of hers had finally started to break her. When on the fifth time back to the stove, she began beating and cursing at it. Sostar was summoned there by the SPIRIT, to make sure the Underworld did not take advantage of her vulnerable state. Yet when he saw Summer Ray crying hysterically, he began to move closer to her. Rory pulled him back and exclaimed to his comrade, "Not yet, Sostar! She must go through this." When Rory saw Summer Ray collapse on the floor, he turned to Sostar and shouted in the spirit world, "Now!"

Immediately Sostar was standing beside Summer Ray, while Rory was crouching beside her with one knee on the floor. When Rory placed a hand on Summer's left shoulder, Summer lifted her tear stained face from being

169

buried in her hands as her Guardian Angel whispered, "Call Pat." Summer then looked up at the counter where her cell phone was and yelled, "Damnit!"

She then rolled over onto her knees, stood up and wiping the tears from her eyes, and she grabbed the cell phone. Leaning against the counter, she opened the phone and searched for Pat's number. Reluctantly dialing, Pat's phone started to ring.

"Hello?" Came a woman's voice on the other end of the line. Summer's asked in a broken voice, "Is this Pat?" Pat politely answered, "Yes, it is."

Summer sounded distant and shy when she said, "Hi, this is Summer Ray. Summer Ray Sherwood. I don't know if you remember me."

Pat happily responded, "Of course I remember you, Honey. I have been hoping every day since I first met you, to hear from you. But by the tone of your voice, something is upsetting you."

Pat then asked, "What is it sweetie? What is troubling you to the point you finally had to break down and call me?" Summer tried the best she could to explain, hoping she didn't sound as crazy as she felt, "It's

170

the stove. I know I have turned it off. I just can't seem to turn it off in my head. I can't make it stop. I keep going back and forth to it."

Pat listening intently finally replied, "Summer, OCD is associated with TBI. You have to learn how to function within your new limitations. I know that is hard for you to hear and why it has taken so long for you to reach out for help. But because you have, it is a sign that you are ready."

Summer got right to the heart of the matter when she replied, "I don't want help. I just want to be normal so I can help myself."

A patient Pat informed her, "Summer, you are normal for who you are NOW. The Summer Ray you used to be is now abnormal. You have to, as I just said, learn how to be normal in a new way and with the new you." Pat tried to enforce only the facts.

Summer exclaimed as she started to cry, "I hate the new me Pat."

Understanding exactly how Summer felt, Pat immediately responded with, "Summer, I hated the new me too. But, when I realized I had no other option, I had

171

to accept it or die. The hardest part of change Summer Ray, is accepting some of those changes do not come with other options." When Summer heard that Pat felt the same way, Summer stopped feeling so alone in her misery and on some far distant planet.

Pat got back to the matters at hand, "Did you use the stove today?"

Summer answered, "No, Ma'am. I almost burnt the house down a few times last week. My friend Kat got really upset with me the other day, and I haven't used it since."

Pat asked, "Do you think burning the house down is a good choice Summer Ray?"

Summer admitted, "No!"

Pat told Summer in a firm and assertive voice, "Then you need to make a better choice to ensure that you and whoever is there at your house are safe. Now, I want you to walk over to the stove."

Summer said, "Okay! I am at the stove."

Pat inquired, "Are there red lights on?"

Summer replied, "No, Ma'am."

Pat continued the questions and asked, "Are all four handles turned to OFF?"

Summer answered, "Yes, Ma'am, they are."

Pat instructed Summer Ray to put her right palm just above a burner, without touching it, then asked, "Do you sense any heat coming from the burners?"

Summer informed Pat, "No! There is no heat."

Pat told Summer, "It is off and you can rest assured the stove cannot hurt you." She then gave Summer further instructions, "Now, walk out of the kitchen and turn off the lights and do not look back." When Summer left the kitchen after turning the light off, the impulse to look back was so strong she had to force herself not to.

Pat almost as if reading her mind said, "Summer Ray, this will take time. Your brain has to get used to the new routine."

"Thank you!" was all Summer could say.

Pat asked, "Where are you now?"

Summer told her, "I am walking upstairs."

Pat inquired with hope in her heart, "Can I call you tomorrow so we can talk about you attending a support group meeting?"

Summer answered, "Sure."

Pat asked one more question, "Great! But until we can get the stove and cooking under control, are you okay with cutting the cord to it so that you cannot use it?"

Summer gave in and said, "I can have Kat's husband cut it tomorrow."

"Excellent," was Pat's response.

Pat ended the conversation expressing her happiness over the fact Summer Ray finally took the first step toward acceptance.

The Angels witnessing a miracle began to speak amongst themselves. It was Luke who spoke up first, "It looks like progress is finally starting to be made."

Rory answered quoting scripture, "Yes! Pride is very destructive for humans. God opposes the proud but gives grace to the humble."

The Warrior Angel Sostar replied, "Praise God that Summer Ray is starting to bend toward that grace."

On her way to her son's room, Summer passed by three Heavenly Hosts watching over her and Billy. When she opened the door to his room, she saw that he was already fast asleep. Their faithful dog Max was on her son's bed stretched out beside him. When he heard Summer Ray open the door, his ears perked up and his tail started wagging. She then walked over to her own room and crawled into her bed. It wasn't long before she too, was fast asleep. Max came in and checked on his mistress before he went to his bed downstairs. Passing by the Angels in the hallway as he headed downstairs, Luke stopped to pet him and said, "Good dog Max."

Rory with a smile replied, "Yes! He makes our job easier."

Sostar then told his comrades, "Godspeed. I must return to Captain Talhelm."

"Godspeed!" Rory and Luke told him.

Thousands of other surrounding Angels sang in unison as Sostar flew out of sight, "Praise be to the Lamb."

CHAPTER NINE

These Honored Dead

On November 17, 1863, President Abraham Lincoln was in Washington, D.C. The good President, while intently working on his famous "Gettysburg Address" speech was also working on the executive order of where the Union Pacific Railroad starting point should be. Omaha, Nebraska became that place. A day later, traveling by rail on a steam engine, through Baltimore, Maryland; New Freedom, Pennsylvania; and Hanover Junction, Pennsylvania; President Lincoln arrived in Gettysburg. He was greeted by cheering crowds as he was there to honor the soldiers that died during the Battle of Gettysburg. Miraculously, while the country was engaged in a great Civil War between the North and South, from East to West a transcontinental railroad was being built.

General Grenville Dodge, a Union General and eventually the chief engineer of the Union Pacific Railroad, when asked to retire from the army to give his full attention to the rail, made the following public statement:

> "*Nothing but the utter defeat of the rebel armies will ever bring peace. I have buried some of my best friends in the South, and I intend to remain there until we can visit their graves under the peaceful protection of that flag that every loyal citizen loves to honor and every soldier fights to save.*"[5]

His wife Anne, also wanted him to resign from the army to join the Union Pacific, and to his wife, General Dodge is quoted saying:

> "*My heart is in the war; Everyday tells me that I am right, and you will see it in the future.*"[5]

Though General Dodge's patriotism was obvious his disdain and hatred for the Indians was also just as evident. He had no consideration for the dilemma the government put the Indians in. Dodge believed:

178

"There were no friendly Indians."[5]

One could understand why he felt such a strong loathing toward them. The Indian war guerillas of the Sioux and the Cheyenne tribes struck the rail lines at a variety of places. War parties derailed trains, killed workers, scalped women, and destroyed hundreds of miles of already laid track. However, the Pawnee and Cherokee Indians did not fit into the same category as the guerillas. Unfortunately, General Dodge did not think so and would soon become a cause of concern for Ms. Summer Ray Sherwood.

The Transformation

President Abraham Lincoln's famous "Gettysburg Address" speech was recited on November 19, 1863 at the Soldiers Cemetery in Gettysburg. Since then, November 19th is Remembrance Day. It is a day to honor and to remember America's soldiers past, present and future. The day is filled with festivities, including the Remembrance Day Ball at the famous Gettysburg Hotel that Summer Ray was attending.

Summer was dressed in a Civil War ball gown that she had bought at the Gettysburg Emporium on Baltimore Street. Eileen, the proprietor, had Summer's gown custom made. When she first walked into the store, Eileen took one look at her and thought she saw a train wreck. Summer's lack of etiquette and proper breeding was quite evident.

"Can I help you Miss?" Eileen asked a disheveled Summer Ray.

"Uh," was all she could reply. Thankfully, her best friend stepped in and said, "She is looking for a gown to wear for the Remembrance Day Ball."

Eileen inquired, "Do you have something in mind?" Seeing the blank look on Summer's face, Eileen graciously added, "Have you ever been to a ball before?" At that point, already knowing the answer, Eileen took charge and told her seamstresses exactly what Summer Ray needed.

All at once the store was abuzz with women bringing Summer Ray items she had never seen before.

Eileen thought to herself, "Oh this is worse than I thought. This one needs some serious help."

Kat, as if reading Eileen's mind said, "Can you please help her? She has no idea what she is supposed to do."

"Yes, Dear, that is quite obvious." Eileen replied, and off to the dressing room she whisked Summer Ray.

A curious Summer asked, "What are we doing?"

"I want you to try on some gowns." Eileen responded in such a way that Summer didn't dare object. After having stripped down to the bare necessities, layer after layer of clothing started to be put on Summer Ray. Summer thought Eileen wasn't strong enough to fling her across the dressing room when she pulled the strings to her corset. Oh how wrong she was.

Eileen instructed Summer, "Now, I want you to reach down and pull up the ladies."

"What ladies?" was Summer's baffled response.

Eileen, being the woman of high class and breeding that she is, gruffly stated, "Your boobs, reach

181

down and pull them up and out so that they can come out and dance." When Summer hesitated Eileen spoke up and warned her, "If you don't pull them up yourself, I will reach down and pull them up myself."

For fear Eileen would make good on her threat, Summer Ray, immediately reached down and began to pull the "ladies" up, and found cleavage she didn't even know she had. When the "ladies" were up to Eileen's satisfaction, Eileen then pulled the already, "I can barely breathe as it is" corset even tighter.

Eileen informed an almost unconscious Summer, "This keeps the ladies from falling back down."

Once Eileen put the gown on her, Summer looked in the mirror, and she could hardly believe her own eyes. Anxiously waiting in the store were Kat and the seamstresses. They knew Eileen had to work a lot of magic to make Summer Ray a "real lady." You know, much like Cinderella and her fairy god mother. When Summer tried to go out of the dressing room the normal way, Eileen asked one of her seamstresses to, "Show her the proper way to exit through a door."

The seamstress then said to Summer, "Turn to the side and grab the bone of the hoop skirt. Walk side by side, until you are clear of the doorway."

When Summer finally made her entrance out into the store, once Katie caught her breath she asked, "Summer Ray Sherwood, is that really you?"

Eileen wasn't finished with Summer, though. When she saw how Summer walked, she immediately stopped her and said, "You do not want to look like a bell Summer Ray, clanging back and forth. You want to look like a lady and glide. Heel, toe, heel, toe. Now try it."

As a figure skater, the "glide" part Summer understood. She immediately self-corrected and began to glide in such a way that it was hard to tell that she had never done that before. Yet, the bubble she was floating on burst when Eileen told her to sit in a chair. Summer didn't have a clue as to how she was supposed to sit in a chair when the clothes she had on were so tight she felt like a robot. Yet, through Eileen's patience and kindness, Summer even learned how to sit like a lady of proper breeding.

When the Remembrance Day Ball finally arrived, Eileen and her staff helped Summer Ray to get dressed at the store. Kathryn Black was eternally grateful. She knew she couldn't pull the strings to Summer's corset as tight as Eileen did without getting punched. Summer had the utmost respect for Eileen and Kat used that knowledge for her own self-preservation. When Eileen saw Summer Ray look down as she was leaving the store, all at once Summer heard Eileen's authoritative voice deepen.

"Summer Ray!" Summer slowly turned around and lifted her head somewhat scared and hesitant,

"Ma'am!" was all she could reply.

"A lady never looks down. She sees where she wants to go and casts her eyes forward. And Summer Ray, you are a very lovely lady." The way Eileen projected that rebuke, Summer felt as if Eileen was proud of her and not really scolding her.

"Yes Ma'am!" Summer said with a smile.

The Remembrance Day Ball

It was November 19th, a cold and crisp, fall evening in Gettysburg. The leaves surrounding the town on the battlefields had changed to beautiful colors of red, orange and yellow. Autumn had indeed adorned the small historical town in all its glory. Although Kathryn Black was not attending the ball, not wanting Summer Ray to back out of at least making an appearance, she decided it was best to stay at the Quality Inn for the night. Upon approaching The Square, a horse drawn carriage pulled in front of them, on their way around the circle to the hotel.

Summer asked, "Who is that?" Kat responded, "It's the Mayor."

Summer kept up the bombardment of questions, "The Mayor of what?"

Kat slowly losing her patience informed Summer, "The Mayor of Gettysburg Summer Ray, Mayor Troxell and his wife, the First Lady."

As Summer started to turn and run she said, "The Mayor of Gettysburg, are you freakin kidding me? He's going to the ball? Oh, no! I can't do this."

Kat inquired as she stopped Summer, "Can't do what?"

A defensive Summer told her friend, "You know I stutter. You know I don't talk right. I cannn't go in there. You know I hate crowds, especially the high society kind. You know I won't fit in."

A now angry Kat responded, "What the hell are you talking about Summer Ray? You know, sometimes I just want to slap you. You have to stop using your accident as an excuse. You can do this. You must do this! Since when did you start giving a crap what people thought of you?"

As other townspeople and tourists looked on, Summer screamed, "Kat, I can't do this."

When Kat put her hands-on Summer's shoulders and said, "Summer, listen to me!" Summer, instantly was lost in thought to a different time and place, where she knew she had heard those words before.

Kat jarred her friend and asked, "Summer Ray?"

"What?" Summer said, not paying attention to the moment at hand.

Kat replied, "Never mind, I will pick you up at midnight."

Summer jokingly responded, "Please make it 11:45. I really don't want to turn back into a pumpkin in front of all those people." As Summer began to walk toward the front entrance of the famous Gettysburg Hotel, the butterflies were fluttering in her stomach so loud, she couldn't even hear her own self think. When she reached the top of the stairs to where a gentleman door greeter was, she was ever so thankful she didn't trip up the stairs and look like the complete idiot she felt like.

The gentleman door greeter politely spoke, "Welcome Ms. Sherwood." Summer didn't say a word. She just looked at him as if he was from planet Mars. Upon walking to the front desk, where the friendly staff greeted her by name, Summer Ray was starting to feel even more uncomfortable and asked, "Could you please direct me to the ball?"

The kind woman at the front desk told her, "Yes, Ma'am. Walk down those stairs, follow around McClellan's to the left and you will see the Grand Ballroom entrance."

187

Summer then exclaimed, "Please call me Summer."

The surprised front desk clerk replied, "Oh no Ms. Sherwood, I cannot do that."

Upon hearing the other staff, calling her by her formal name as well, it made Summer Ray even more nervous. She looked down at her gown thinking Katie placed a sticker on her with her name on it. You know, like they do in elementary school for little kids. No! Summer Ray would not put it passed Kat to do such a thing. But nope, there was no sticker.

As Summer walked down the stairs and past McClellan's in her cumbersome ball gown, she instantly remembered what Eileen said back at the Gettysburg Emporium. "Heel, toe, heel, toe" and repeated it softly to herself out loud. This way she could walk in unison to those words.

When she walked through the atrium, all at once, Summer was immersed in Civil War ambiance. Arriving at the entrance to the Grand Ballroom the Banquet Captain approached her.

Jozalyn, the plump Banquet Captain with curly red hair asked, "May I have your name Miss?"

Summer graciously replied, "My name is Summer Ray Sherwood."

Jozalyn informed her, "Finally, Miss Sherwood. I have been expecting you."

Summer wondering what in the world was going on just had to ask, "Wait! What? Why have you been expecting me?"

Off in the background Summer heard, "Oh look, she's a spinster."

Summer turned to look at who called her that and was surprised to see a group of very young women all dressed up with wedding rings on. With Summer having Traumatic Brain Injury, she was not always rational or reasonable, especially in the areas of being misunderstood or made fun of. So she immediately started to walk towards the group, when Summer was abruptly stopped by Jozalyn, "Oh no Ms. Sherwood, you mustn't do that. It would not be ladylike at all."

Summer said in her defense, "But they just called me a "spinster."

Jozalyn gently replied hoping to prevent a brawl, "To them you ARE a spinster." She continued to intervene trying to diffuse the situation but only creating a new one when she stated, "Here, let me introduce you to the Matron Duvall." Summer did not realize she was about to be thrown to an entire pack of wolves in the form of just one human. The reason being that the Matron Duvall was worse than all those girls put together.

Jozalyn continued, "She will be your escort for the evening."

Summer Ray demanded to know, "Escort? Why do I need an escort?"

The savvy Banquet Captain took charge and pronounced, "Matron Duvall, I would like to introduce you to Ms. Summer Ray Sherwood, great-great granddaughter of General Richard S. Sherwood."

As the Matron curtseyed, Summer Ray asked, "What is she doing?" Then began to frantically speak, "She is freaking me out. How do you know who I am? How does anyone know?"

Summer's lack of awareness of her surroundings was starting to get to her. And as if to taunt Summer Ray, the Matron Duvall pulled out a little pocket book from her reticule and began to flip through the pages.

Turning to Summer Ray, the Matron sharply spoke, "You are not married are you Ms. Sherwood? From the looks of things, like those lines around your eyes, you are over the age of 25 and you are here without an escort. Am I right in my assessment, Ms. Sherwood?" The Matron did not wait for an answer from Summer and continued, "According to the Pipestone Civil War Days Committee, in their book, '*The Victorian and Civil War Era Weddings*,'[7]

'*Unmarried people were considered pitiful burdens.*'

The Pipestone Committee also state in their book:

'*The common belief during the Victorian era was there was little hope for happiness without a mate. This was especially the case for an unmarried woman, who was viewed as not fulfilling their duty to marry. They were looked*

*down by members of the community, unless they
were independently wealthy and of good
character.*[7]

'*Young ladies were usually married by the age of
twenty and were considered spinsters if they
remained unmarried at the age of twenty-five.*[7]

In the Victorian Era, it is also proper behavior to
curtsey at every formal introduction. It is called,
'etiquette.' You do know what 'etiquette' is, do you not
Ms. Sherwood?"

The Matron did not know how close she came to
getting Summer's rather strong, right skating leg kicked
down her throat, after such a public display of mockery.

Summer answered in a very perturbed and
agitated voice, "Of course I know what 'etiquette' is."

"Unless you are a gentleman, you are to curtsey
at any formal introduction. Do you understand me, Ms.
Sherwood?" The Matron instructed her as fire was
starting to come out of Summer's eyes, and how Summer
wished it was real fire.

The Matron was a larger and much older woman than Summer. She had on a bright green and orange flowered ball gown made of cotton and not silk. The Matron Duvall was holding a fan, wearing a shawl, wore long white gloves and her blonde hair could barely be seen underneath her navy bonnet. She had hazel green eyes and big rosy red cheeks. Summer wanted to rip those cheeks right off her face. Instead, Summer excused herself, telling the Matron she needed to use the ladies room. When Summer tripped while walking toward the ladies rest room, one of the other young married girls said, "What a klutz." The rest of the conversation between the five of them went something like this,

"Oh look, she is even wearing red laced pantaloons."

"Who invited her here?"

"Did you see her nails? They are red too."

"Only loose women wear red."

"What boat did she just step off of?"

193

The Best You

As Summer continued to hear the bombardment of insults from these so called ladies of breeding, a tear or two could be seen as she threw her reticule on the bathroom counter. Her rough and tough exterior could no longer hide the tenderness inside a heart that was easily wounded.

Thinking she was alone, Summer whispered to herself, "I told Kat I couldn't do this."

An unfamiliar voice spoke behind her, "Can't do what my dear?"

As Summer slowly turned toward the voice, she almost fainted when she saw who it was.

Summer could barely get the words out, "Aren't...aren't you Rosa Parks?"

Rosa asked, avoiding Summer's obvious shock at her presence, "Yes, I am! But you did not answer my question. What can't you do?"

Summer sadly replied, "This lady stuff, it just isn't me."

Rosa Parks inquired as she came to stand next to Summer Ray, "So, let me get this straight. You can teach

Special Needs children how to ice skate, but you cannot be a woman of breeding and of high social status. Is that what I am hearing? In other words, what you are really trying to say is that you are no good at being stuck up."

Summer asked in a curious manner, "How do you know I'm a Figure Skater?"

Rosa was vague, "Someone thought you might need *another* fairy godmother." Rosa continued, "Summer Ray, to achieve with a disability you must recognize your limitations. Look at what you can do, instead of what you cannot. Once you accept your disabilities, you can ascend your abilities."

Summer, still defensive, replied, "You heard those girls in there. I don't fit in."

Rosa Parks asked, "Tell me, Summer Ray, when I chose to sit at the front of the bus and not the back, did I fit in?"

A humbled Summer answered, "No, Ma-am. You helped to change the course of history."

Rosa exclaimed, to a now almost crying Summer Ray, "My disability was not due to an accident like yours.

I was born a colored woman in a white man's world. My limitation was the color of my skin, but it was not the color of my heart. In the famous words of Eleanor Roosevelt,

'No-one can make you feel inferior without your consent.'

The disturbing truth about slavery and racism, Summer Ray, is that the skin may have been white, but the heart was black."

"I am so sorry," was all Summer could reply.

Rosa responded with amazing character, "Don't be. Look at us now. An African American is President and slavery has long since been abolished, at least in this country. Though, sad to say, racism has crossed over the boundaries to Mexicans and Latinos, as well as the Blacks. This is the same country where 'all men are created equal.' Where men and woman, since its conception, have fought, bled and died for its freedom. The scourge of racism lives on, even if slavery does not."

Summer, feeling helpless, asked, "What do I do?"

Rosa replied with a sparkle in her eyes, "You be the best you that you can be. Be who you were created by God to be, not who others think you should be. Why do you want to fit into the mold of others, Summer Ray? God allowed your accident for a reason. You have to learn how to accept yourself, therefore the opinions of others won't cause you so many angry and instant harmful responses. It only gives them more fuel for the fire and you only reinforce their bad opinions, without really wanting to. You see Summer Ray, having a head injury such as yours, you are more easily frustrated and easily angered. Don't be! Because what you feel are your greatest weaknesses, God has turned and made them your greatest strengths.

Now wipe your eyes. The Colonel Michael Moses McDaniels is waiting to dance with you. You will be the envy of all those girls, single, betrothed and married."

As Summer Ray turned to inquire of this Colonel McDaniels, Rosa Parks suddenly vanished.

When Summer Ray came back to the foyer of the Grand Ballroom, it was with a newly found freedom herself.

The perturbed and agitated Matron Duvall instructed her, "You, Ms. Sherwood, are not to leave my side. If a gentleman asks you to dance, you give him the honor of your hand."

Without waiting for an answer, the Matron ordered Jozalyn to open the door to the Grand Ballroom. Summer could hardly believe her eyes. The first thing she noticed was the twenty-eight-foot ceiling. It was the original ceiling from the 1800's – 1814 to be exact. The ceiling was hand painted green and burgundy, with real gold chips sprinkled in. The chandeliers were 19th century and the velvet drapes looked as if they were emeralds. Looking to her left, Summer saw a massive vault that was beyond description and the marble floor that was there since the building's construction. After a battle of such magnitude and such great proportions as the Battle of Gettysburg, Summer was amazed at how the bank had been preserved so beautifully.

Standing by the American flag, a certain Colonel in his dress Union uniform had been waiting anxiously for his "scrawny young woman" to appear. Suddenly his attention was once again fixated on her. When the Colonel saw Summer walk into the Grand Ballroom he was mesmerized. If a ghost could breathe, he was definitely breathing heavy at the sight of her. Her taffeta gown was teal blue with a white baroque bodice. Her short ruffled and lace sleeves were worn off the shoulders and exposed the "ladies" that many a men standing nearby admired. She wore white gloves, just to her wrists to cover her tattoo, and her long black hair was curled and pulled up under a matching snood. Her pearl earrings sparkled, and a pink and white cameo necklace adorned her neck.

When she gracefully walked into the Grand Ballroom, the Colonel McDaniels noticed the Matron Duvall and grimaced. He then said, "It looks like I will have to go through the Master of Ceremonies and the over gregarious Matron Duvall if I hope to dance with Ms. Summer Ray Sherwood."

Off in the distance, the devious General Dodge also noticed Summer Ray. As his eyes fell across her face, he instantly knew she was a half breed. The blood in his

199

veins had already begun to boil when he noticed Colonel McDaniels approach the Matron Duvall.

As final introductions finished between Summer Ray and the receiving line, the Matron Duvall escorted Summer to their dinner table. When Summer Ray reached for her cell phone in her purse, she found it wasn't there. Summer Ray was glued to her cell phone. The fact that it was missing was almost impossible, but not so impossible if cell phones hadn't been invented yet. Summer was about to call Kat to have her pick her up early.

Not wanting to be rude, Summer tried to excuse herself as politely as she could from the Matron Duvall only to be chastised with, "My dear, I have told you, a unaccompanied woman such as yourself, is not to leave a ball unescorted. It is bad manners and bad breeding to do so."

A bewildered Summer asked, "What is up with all this bad manners and bad breeding stuff? Don't you think you are taking this reenacting stuff just a little too far Ms. Duvall? People don't talk like you in the 21st

200

century!" Jozalyn gasped. The Matron sternly stated, "It is Matron!"

As Summer Ray looked around the ball room, she noticed there were not any re-enactors dressed as Confederate Generals, other officers or even soldiers for that matter. She only saw Union officers in their dress uniforms. To her astonishment, she also saw what looked like real servants. Summer was beginning to wonder what planet she was on, let alone what state she was in.

"Is this not the Remembrance Day Ball?" Summer was reluctant to ask anyone in attendance but herself. Just then, a man who Summer thought she recognized as the same man who showed her where Jack Skelly's grave was, came to the Matron Duvall and politely asked the Matron if he could dance with Summer.

The Matron firmly informed him, "Not without a formal introduction Colonel McDaniels!"

Before a startled Summer could respond and speak for herself, once again the Matron Duvall spoke,

"Ms. Summer Ray Sherwood, this is Colonel Michael Moses McDaniels of the Union Army of the

Potomac. He has requested to dance with you. Your dance card has him listed as #1 for a waltz."

Summer asked, "Dance card? What dance card?"

The Matron snapped, "The one in your reticule, get it out!" As Summer opened her reticule, she was stunned to see the dance card and was even more shocked when she opened it. Inside the dance card was a list of Union officers' names written on it and sure enough, Colonel McDaniels was indeed listed as number one, just as the Matron said.

As the Colonel bowed to Summer Ray, the Matron reminded Summer to curtsey at any formal introduction. An unenthusiastic Summer obliged and curtseyed to the Colonel. A bemused Colonel then inquired, "May I have the pleasure of your hand for this waltz Ms. Sherwood?"

Summer conversed to herself, "Anything to get away from this pain in the ass woman!"

As Summer Ray put out her right hand to give it to the Colonel, knowing it would hurt if he grabbed onto it too hard, she abruptly pulled back.

202

The Colonel, already aware of her injured hand, said to Summer, "I can assure you, Ms. Sherwood, I am a gentleman. I will not hurt your hand."

Reluctantly, Summer put her hand in his and as she tried to speak, not wanting to harm neither his nor Summer's reputation, the Colonel said, "Not yet, Miss Sherwood, not with the Matron watching so intently. She will proceed to embarrass us both as not being properly bred."

As they began to dance a waltz, the Colonel noticed how elegantly Summer could move across the dance floor, and how she poised herself like a true woman of breeding.

The Colonel told himself, "Well, at least she carries herself like a woman of quality."

Summer explained, "Years and years of dance practice."

The curious Colonel asked her, "You read minds too?"

Summer shot back, "Oh, I am allowed to speak now?"

He informed a now disturbed Summer, "You know, women back in my day were not as forthright as you are."

Summer spoke, "Forthright? Are you freakin kidding me? You know, people don't talk that anymore." She continued, "What do you mean, your day?"

The Colonel shot back, "Do you always ask so many questions Ms. Sherwood?"

Summer didn't miss a beat, "Do you always avoid answering questions, Mr. McDaniels? What do you mean 'your day'?"

Her questions continued, "Why do you have on two uniforms? When I first saw you standing by the American Flag, you were wearing a Colonel's uniform."

The quizzical present-day General asked, "You noticed me?"

"Well, you are sort of like a Union Rhett Butler you know! You are hard to miss. Besides, you are the same man who showed me Jack Skelly's gravesite, are you not, Colonel? Or is it General McDaniels?" a now frustrated Summer asked him.

The General replied, "Yes! I did show you where Jack Skelly's grave was located."

Summer thankfully said, "Wow! Thank God. I was beginning to think you were a ghost, or that I was seeing things." She then continued her barrage of questions, "Why are there no Confederates here and above all, why are there workers here who look like they are slaves? There shouldn't be slaves in Gettysburg or slaves anywhere for that matter. The war is over is it not Colonel McDaniels, or is it General McDaniels?" Summer finally allowed him to get a word in edgewise. "Two uniforms, is that what you now see? And it is 'General'."

The General was only interested in few of Summer Ray's questions when he said, "Tell me Ms. Sherwood,"

"Please stop calling me that. Call me Summer or Summer Ray," an irritated Summer blurted.

The General continued, "Tell me, then, Summer Ray, who is standing over there by the bar, with a cigar in his mouth?" General McDaniels asked Summer as he turned her to see the bar, while still dancing a waltz. Even

205

from far away, Summer could tell it was none other than General Ulysses S. Grant, cigar and all.

Summer expressed to the General, "Wow! The resemblance is amazing."

General McDaniels then asked Summer Ray, "Your last name is Sherwood. Is that any relation to General Richard S. Sherwood?"

Summer proudly informed him, "He is my great-great grandfather."

The questions by the General continued, "Then who is that standing over there by the buffet table laughing with his wife?"

A now defiant Summer asked, "Why so many questions Mr. McDaniels?"

He replied in a firm, not haughty voice, "It is 'General'."

Summer responded, "And to answer your 100th question, that man looks like my great-great grandfather."

A prying General asked, "Do you not find it odd that he and you are here at the same time?"

Summer said laughing, "They are re-enactors General McDaniels, just like you are. What is so odd about it? The Matron Duvall, now that's odd."

General prodded Summer, "Look again and this time look closer."

As Summer dropped her arms from his, she began to walk toward General Sherwood and his wife.

She was unexpectedly stopped by her dance partner who asked, "What are you doing? I told you to look closer, not get closer."

Summer responded with an intensity the General hadn't seen before, "Let go of me! The only way I can look closer, is if I get closer!"

"Summer Ray, you just cannot go barging in on a conversation without being properly introduced, especially not with a General, for God's sake." General McDaniels said, knowing already it was pointless to try to reason with her.

Summer angrily yelled back to him, "Your habits and mannerisms are outdated beyond belief!"

The General knew Summer Ray was not in his time period of the 19th century, but in her own and wasn't about to listen to any more of his "outdated habits and mannerisms" as she called them. Still, knowing Summer Ray was about to be confronted with the shock of her life, the Colonel/General knew it was best to stand behind an about to be fainting Summer.

As she approached her distant great-great grandparents something was terribly amiss, and Summer could sense it. With the General close at hand, Summer Ray was finally beginning to unlock the mystery of the distorted evening that should have been an enchanted one.

"Hello, my name is Summer Ray. Could you please enlighten General," Summer looked back at him and saw the General's uniform had suddenly changed back to a Colonel's uniform, "Uh Colonel McDaniels here..." Summer was cut off by the Colonel.

He humbly spoke as he nodded to General Sherwood, "I apologize for this outburst, General, Sir. Ms. Sherwood is not used to our customs."

Summer demanded to know, "What customs?"

An exasperated Summer then told the Colonel, "You act as if this is the *REAL* General Sherwood and as if they are my *REAL* great-great grandparents."

General Sherwood asked the Colonel who this peculiar woman was.

The Colonel McDaniels made formal introductions, "Ms. Summer Ray Sherwood, I would like to introduce you to General Richard S. Sherwood and his lovely wife, Lady Elizabeth."

Lady Sherwood told Summer, "Pleased to make your acquaintance. We have the same last name, my dear."

Summer gasped, barely able to get the words out, "You two look an awful lot like my father's real great grandparents."

All at once the realization that she was talking to her real great-great grandmother overpowered her and she did exactly what the Colonel anticipated – she fainted. The Colonel caught Summer in his arms and carried her to a couch outside the ballroom in the atrium. As he was carrying Summer, the General in present day, remembered how he had lifted her to her feet at Big

Round Top, and how he held her in his arms as he helped Katie to get her down the hill. He could hardly believe this was the same scrawny young woman he had met ten years earlier. But here, once again, Summer Ray was in his arms.

When the Matron Duvall saw him carry a lifeless Summer out of the ballroom she followed him and bellowed out, "What happened to her?"

The Matron demanded to know had happened, as she began to fan Summer's face.

The General McDaniels responded, "She met the *REAL* Sherwoods and as you can see Matron Duvall, she fainted."

The Matron flatly told him, "I knew she could not be tamed. She is too undomesticated."

Defending Summer the General replied, "Ms. Sherwood is not from our time and did not know any better. I tried to stop her. But without drawing unwanted attention to ourselves, I had to let her meet them. Was that not the gentlemanly thing to do Matron Duvall?"

In Matron Duvall's French overbearing tone, she angrily replied, "Hogwash!"

She then stormed out of the atrium and went back into the ballroom. The General knelt down beside Summer Ray and took off her bonnet. Her coal black hair fell around her face and he couldn't help but notice her high cheek bones.

He thought to himself, "Cherokee! I will have to make sure the conniving General Dodge does not get a hold of her."

General McDaniels then brushed some of Summer's black hair away from her face.

As Summer Ray began to slowly open her eyes, it was like she was trying to see through a hazy fog. There was a man kneeling beside her. Yet he was bloody, dusty, wounded, and he had on both a Union and Confederate General's uniform. Summer thought she was hallucinating. But when she reached out to touch his face, she could feel that he wasn't just a hallucination. He was real.

Summer softly asked, "Who are you?"

The General, as she saw him in present day, took the white glove off her right hand and gently kissed the scars where the thorns dug deep into her palm.

The General then looked at Summer Ray with tears of anguish in his eyes and pleaded, "Please, Summer Ray Sherwood, please remember your promise!"

Back to Gettysburg

"Remember your promise!" Summer immediately woke up out of her slumber asking, "What promise?"

She repeated the words over and over again, until she finally regained full consciousness.

"Colonel Michael McDaniels - his name is Colonel McDaniels." Summer said out loud. As she sat on her bed, biting her well-manicured nails, she pondered the dream she just had.

"That was too real to not be true!" Summer told herself.

She didn't waste time. Summer scurried out of bed and ran downstairs, almost tripping over her dog on the way to her office.

"Sorry Max!" Summer told her German Shepherd.

Max, being used to his mistress' antics, didn't budge! He just wagged his tail as if to say, "It's okay. I am used to it. But I love you anyway!"

Once at her computer she moved the mouse to wake it up. Summer had to get to her internet and do research on this Colonel Michael McDaniels. She had to know if he was real or if it was "just a dream."

Thinking out loud she yelled, "Come on, come on! You are a slow piece of @#$%%^!"

Summer was never godly when she was impatient. "Finally!" she said.

She did a search on Colonel Michael Moses McDaniels.

MILITARY SERVICE - GETTYSBURG
Colonel Michael Moses McDaniels
The Army of the Potomac

Served under General Meade

DEATH

July 2, 1863.

Wheat Field Gettysburg, PA

Gravesite...The Gettysburg National Cemetery

Gettysburg, PA

PERSONAL

Born August 16, 1833

Death July 2, 1863

Divorced – June 1, 1863

Lily McDaniels - remarried

No children

Summer looked up Lily McDaniels hoping to get some kind of historical information such as what she looked like or family genealogy. It's possible the General was mistaking Summer for Lily.

Summer asked out loud, "Is that the promise he was talking about – a promise of fidelity perhaps? Has his ghost come back to haunt the women of Gettysburg, due to his lost love? No, that doesn't even make sense."

She then said, "He had on two uniforms, one of a Confederate Soldier and one of a Union Soldier, and he was now a General. Why was he a Colonel then, if he had on...?" Summer drifted off thinking.

Tomorrow morning could not get there fast enough, but the timing was perfect. Billy was going camping for two weeks with his dad and that would give Summer Ray plenty of time for research. Summer was going back to Gettysburg to find a ghost, a real ghost. Yet she knew she wasn't going alone. Looking at the clock on her computer that read 2:30AM, Summer whispered, "Oh she *IS* going to kill me."

It was the early hour of the phone call that prompted Kat to grasp the seriousness in Summer's voice.

"Summer, are you okay? It is 2:30 in the morning. What is wrong? Are you sick? Is Billy okay?"

As Kat began to ask a thousand questions, Summer stopped her in mid-sentence and said, "Yes! We are fine. I promise to tell you everything if you come to Gettysburg with me tomorrow. We have to spend the night, so please ask Dave if he wouldn't mind watching Ella. We have to leave by noon."

Kat said to her friend, "You know I love you right?"

Summer replied, "Yes! I know you love me. I will pick you up at noon."

With that the phone went dead and Summer Ray began to sense this was no ordinary trip back to Gettysburg. She had no idea, nor could she have ever imagined, what awaited her there. Had she of known beforehand, she may have chosen to stay home.

CHAPTER TEN

The Camping Trip

An impatient Summer asked her son, "Billy, are you ready? Your dad is almost here."

"Yes!" Billy said as he began to repack his camping gear and continued, "I was just making sure you packed everything."

Summer replied, "Billy, we went over that list a hundred times. What could you possibly think we forgot to pack?"

A shy but truthful Billy said, "Well Mom, you are sort of forgetful?"

"Point taken Son, point taken!" Summer had to agree.

Just then, the doorbell rang, and it was Tommy, Billy's dad. Summer never liked these halfhearted kid exchanges between her and her ex-husband. They just were never a happy one. But with Billy being so excited about his camping trip, Summer was excited for him and did not want to muddy the waters.

Summer said to her ex-husband, "Hello Tom. Billy made sure I didn't forget anything."

"Thank you!" an indifferent Tommy answered her.

"Come on Billy, let's get your gear." His dad instructed his son and off to the garage they both went.

With the truck packed, Billy ran back to the front step to hug and kiss his momma goodbye. Suddenly, the tears began to fall from Summer's eyes as it was going to be two long weeks without her adorable son.

Seeing Summer's sad expression, an angry Tommy yelled, "Summer Ray! Stop it. You will make Billy feel bad!"

Wiping the tears from her eyes, Summer told her son, "You know I love you Son, be careful and don't forget to call me every night."

As Billy started to run back toward the truck he yelled out, "Well, maybe not every night. But I will call you sometime! Love you too, Mom."

Summer waved goodbye from the porch and went back inside before her son and ex-husband left the driveway. Summer's accident almost left her irrational and extremely overprotective of Billy, especially while he was traveling. Tommy knew it and it was a source of contention between him and Summer. Tom was relieved when he saw that she had gone back inside as fast as she did. Fighting was no way to start off a summer vacation for their son!

As Summer shut the front door behind her, she silently prayed, "Father God, please keep my Billy safe. Give him traveling mercies. You know how hard it is for me to see him get into a car. You know how hard it is for me to let him out of my sight."
Just then she thought she heard a still and quiet voice inside her, "Trust me."

Though Summer believed in Angels, she just wished she could see them from time to time. But then, she would always tell herself, if she COULD see them, "I guess it wouldn't be faith."

Luke flew off beside Billy, faithfully watching over him on his camping trip. Even with Rory standing beside Summer, for some reason, she still felt alone. Not knowing how the day would progress, Summer had hoped it would at least be a productive one.

219

The Gettysburg National Cemetery

Summer and Kat checked into the Inn at Cemetery Hill on Baltimore Street at 1:00PM. Shirley, the smiling and welcoming guest clerk asked the ladies, "May I help you?"

Summer replied, "Yes, please. We have a reservation under Summer Ray Sherwood."

The guest clerk then said to the ladies, "We have your reservation. But I do apologize that room will not be ready until 2:00PM."

Summer kindly responded, "That's okay!" Then she asked, "Can we have two room key cards please?"

"Sure! I just need your credit card to swipe the credit card machine," Shirley said. As Summer handed her credit card over the counter, the clerk continued, "We will slip the bill under the door to your room after midnight. If you decide to extend your stay, just feel free to call the front desk. Is there anything else I can help you ladies with right now?"

Summer replied, "No, thank you."

Once back outside the motel, Kat asked, "Are you hungry? What do you want to do? We have an hour to kill." As the two ladies walked up Baltimore Street toward the National Cemetery, they saw a sign that read, "*Civil War Tails at the Homestead....Diorama Museum.*" Summer saw the sign had an outline of a cat and said, "Come on, Cat Lady. This I have got to see."

Upon entering the museum, they were met by two of the nicest people on the planet, Rebecca and Ruth. They were twin sisters fulfilling their lifelong dream of living in Gettysburg and sharing their love of history and cats all at the same time. It truly was a remarkable museum. There were thousands upon thousands of handmade tiny Civil War Union and Confederate soldier cats hand-made out of clay and housed in displays of Gettysburg battles. Rebecca had bought the Old Orphanage and rented part of it, to some really cool tenants who apparently were treated like family.

Back outside Summer stopped short so fast that Kat ran right into her and asked, "Summer what is with you?"

But Summer was lost in thought. Without realizing it, three ghost children ran right in front of her; two girls and a boy were laughing and playing. As the

221

ghost children ran toward Mrs. Humiston, the hair on Summer's head blew in a soft gentle breeze, while Kat's hair stood still. With Kat being the "paranormal" one, you would be the other way around. Thankfully, the cemetery was just a block from the museum.

Upon walking into the entrance of The Gettysburg National Cemetery on Baltimore Street, both Summer and her friend could feel they were on historical, sacred and hallowed ground. The afternoon sun was hot with the temperature around 90 degrees. Both Summer and Kat had on shorts and sandals. Kat was wearing short sleeved tunic shirt almost covering her shorts, while Summer had on, as usual, a tank top! Summer Ray never liked to draw attention to herself, never realizing that is exactly what she did.

Upon seeing some of the markers of the US Unknown Soldiers as only numbers, Summer became irate. It was a good thing there were not others within earshot or Summer quite possibly would have been thrown out. It was, after all, a National Cemetery where respect for the dead was a requirement and just plain good manners! Not to mention there was a plaque posted that read, "Silence and Respect."

"These are US Soldiers! They are not numbers! Why are they marked only as numbers? This is wrong!" Summer screamed at Kat, as if she knew the answer to her question.

The Lt. Colonel George Jameson was out scouting the town of Gettysburg. Upon seeing Summer at the National Cemetery, he immediately reported back to General McDaniels. Saluting him, he said, "General, Sir, *THAT* woman and her friend are at the National Cemetery and *THAT* woman is yelling."

Within seconds, the General along with a few of his Unknowns, were at The Gettysburg National Cemetery, though invisible to any human. They could only be seen by the dark powers and the Light ones as well.

Summer expressed to her friend, "Okay Katie! We are looking for a Colonel Michael Moses McDaniels, at least I think we are. He was also a General wearing a Union and Confederate uniform. Go figure that one out! You look on this half of the cemetery and

223

I will take the other half over there by that...statue. Wow, is that ever impressive!"

Out of nowhere, an elderly man dressed in a light blue uniform with white hair and a long white beard told them, "The statue is called 'The Genius of Liberty.' It stands 65 feet in the air and was made in Italy. Walk with me. I will show you the other side."

Kat ducked out and said, "You walk with him, Summer. I will search for the Colonel over there."

She pointed toward the trees as Summer gave her a rather hellacious look of, "I *AM* going to kill you." Walking slowly with the man who introduced himself as only "The Gatekeeper," Summer was awestruck by his wealth of knowledge about the Civil War. When they reached the 'Genius of Liberty' the elderly man began to speak, "Standing on top, high above is a woman called 'Genius of Liberty.' The others, two men and two women represent, 'war,' 'peace,' 'history,' and 'plenty'."

"Wow! They look like they can see right through us," exclaimed Summer Ray.

With a twinkle in his eye The Gatekeeper replied, "It is Gettysburg, my dear. It is Gettysburg.

Speaking of which, there is a plaque of Lincoln's 'Gettysburg Address' right beside the statue. It was not, however, the actual place where Lincoln gave his famous speech. That was in The Evergreen Cemetery."

Across the cemetery, Kat yelled out to her friend, "Summer, I found it over here!"

When Summer turned around to thank The Gatekeeper, he was gone.

"What is it Dorothy said in the 'Wizard of Oz,' about how people come and go so quickly?" She said to herself as she was walking across the cemetery grass toward her friend.

When Summer came upon the gravestone she bent down and said, "Colonel Michael Moses McDaniels. Wow! There he is." The General, upon seeing Summer touch his name on his gravestone, knew beyond the shadow of a doubt that this was, in fact, the same woman who promised him she would be back all those years before. Right beside the General's gravestone marker on both sides were US Unknown Soldiers.

"Well at least some of the Unknowns are actually US Unknowns, unlike those with just numbers or the words '411 Bodies!' How can they just be numbers? Even if they are just body parts, they are still US Soldiers!" bemoaned Summer.

Kat demanded, "Okay Summer! What is going on? You promised me you would tell me everything." As Summer stood back up, she looked at her anxiously awaiting, almost heat exhausted friend, and tried the best she could to explain what was almost unexplainable!

"I had a dream last night about a Colonel Michael Moses McDaniels. I do not know who he is or why I would dream about him, but he said the words 'remember your promise' and then I woke up. I do not know what promise he is talking about. After I woke up from that dream, I ran to my computer and looked him up on the internet, and sure enough he was a real Colonel. But in my dream, he was wearing both a Confederate and Union uniform, and he was a General. It's all so confusing."

Summer forgot to mention the fact he was the same man who had helped her to find Jack Skelly's grave.

She continued, "I honestly do not know what is going on. But as you can see by his gravestone, he was a

226

real man who fought in the Civil War. I thought he might have mistaken me for his ex-wife Lily. How could I have ever made a promise to a man who existed in the 19th Century?"

When Summer asked her friend that last question a disgruntled General Michael Moses McDaniels, overhearing the conversation, immediately left in a huff with the Lt. Colonel and the Unknowns following close at hand.

"Okay Summer! Let's get to the motel. Maybe a half hour in the hot tub will help you relax." Kat said as she noticed her friend rubbing her head!

Summer complained, "Another migraine, as soon as I try to remember! I hate it."

Back at the motel, Summer grabbed as many brochures about Gettysburg as she could and opened one pertaining to ghost tours.

Summer spoke, "Wow Kat! This sounds really cool. We've got to go on one of these tours."

A worried Kat asked, "So you mean to tell me we are looking for a REAL ghost named Michael Moses McDaniels?"

Summer replied, "What better way to find him! From the looks of these brochures, these are experienced ghost people. Besides aren't you the one who is always telling me to keep an open mind about the paranormal? Come on, it'll be fun,"

Katie reminded Summer, "I tell you to keep an open mind to the fact that ghosts and spirits actually do exist. I tend to leave locating them to the experts without any involvement from me."

Kat was thinking her friend was getting into this ghost stuff just a little too much. But she was there to support Summer, regardless.

Kat unlocked the door to their motel room and Summer immediately threw her overnight bag on one of the double beds and went into the bathroom where the hot tub was.

Summer happily screamed out to her friend, "Wow! This hot tub is awesome."

Kat shouted back, "Okay! Well, don't go under. I don't want to have to explain that you drowned in a hot tub to your son. I can see the headlines now:

Summer Ray Sherwood Survives Massive Car Wreck. But Drowns In A Hot Tub..."

They had only been in Gettysburg for an hour and Kat was already exhausted.

"Yeah! Yeah! Yeah!" was Summer's only response as she slammed the bathroom door.

CHAPTER ELEVEN

Harsh Reality

To some, Gettysburg is a town of invincibility. There is an aura of not being capable of being overcome or conquered. The dark powers find this most amusing as they use such individuals as pawns in their nasty game of death and destruction. Gettysburg is like an island unto itself, where an assorted few are disillusioned into thinking they can escape the harsh realities of the real world.

Be that as it may, the real world still existed within its boundaries. An alcoholic or drug addict would suffer the same consequences inside the town of Gettysburg as outside of the town such as jail, ailing health, insanity and loss of life. Even an enabler cannot stop the decay and deterioration of an abuser of drugs and alcohol. But thankfully, the mercy of Father God can.

At the Battle of Gettysburg, in a three-day heartless and cruel battle, there were over 51,000 casualties. Yet, how many countless other casualties have there been since the war, due to drug and alcohol abuse? Summer Ray's older brother, sister-in-law and cousin died so young, for such stupid addictions. No amount of talking to them ever did any good. They just refused to listen. Even when Summer and other family members and friends pleaded with them to get help, their pleas fell on deaf ears. One died of congestive heart failure due to severe weight loss, one died of a brain hemorrhage and the other died from respiratory distress.

The horrors of war are not just confined to a battlefield of land. Millions of wars are fought every second of every day at home, fighting for a loved one to make the right choices. Though not an excuse, only an alcoholic or a drug addict can understand how those choices can eventually be made for them. Over time, they become slaves to their own addictions. Everyone knows, especially a slave, that he or she is subservient to the master that controls them. Slaves are not permitted to choose. Does it make more sense that such self-abuse could become an illness? Where the alcoholic or drug addict are no longer termed "bad" but "sick?" There's an old tombstone at the Winchester Cathedral in England that has etched into it these words of poetry:

> "Here lies a Hampshire Grenadier,
> who caught his death
> Drinking cold small beer.
> A good soldier is ne'er forget
> Whether he dieth by musket, Or by pot."

It is a proven fact that some alcoholics and drug addicts do die. Summer Ray Sherwood can attest to that fact. Ever since she was a teenager, it has been a harsh reality of life for her.

Where Are All the General Lee's?

During the summer months Gettysburg is a town of celebration and social gathering. It is full of life and for a handful of people a fantasy and a dream come true. The horse drawn carriage ride makes you feel as if love is a possibility, even if you are alone without someone special riding beside you. The costumes from days of old saturate you with a time when chivalry wasn't dead. The preservation of history allows you to forget all of your present-day troubles as you become engrossed in the adventures of the past. It could be for these reasons that the illusion of one is being invincible still settles on the town of Gettysburg. But wasn't it the famous General Robert E. Lee who, because of Pickett's Charge, said the words:

> *"It's all my fault. I thought my men were invincible."*[10]

Those words defined his character. Instead of passing the blame to one of his officers, though General Longstreet tried to reason with the good General, General Lee accepted the responsibility and held himself accountable for the loss at Gettysburg after his planned failed miserably. How sad that so many men lost their lives. How commendable the great General Robert E. Lee left an example of his moral fiber that the world today is in such desperate need of.

Is General Lee not the same man who, after the war was over, while attending church went and kneeled beside a black man at the altar? When the rest of the white congregation just sat there in what appeared to be outrage at that black man's courage and audacity, General Lee made a public and bold display of unity.

Oh, where are all the General Lee's? His mistakes could never overtake his humanity, kindness, charity and moral character. Summer, though strictly a "Yankee," often wondered if General Lee's heart wasn't really sick, but heartbroken instead. The weight of seeing so much bloodshed and death, the war must have shattered any heart that was full of humility, gentleness and compassion.

Summer even heard a story of how General Lee dismounted his horse Traveller and right there in the midst of battle, picked up a helpless little bird and placed it safely back in its nest. If the General's sympathy crossed to the depths of helpless birds, how much more would it have crossed the oceans of dying men? Yes! Summer was

235

certain the heavy weight of war crushed the tender heart of the infamous and legendary General Robert E. Lee.

The Town of Gettysburg

Summer and Kat decided to venture out into the night life of the historical town of Gettysburg. It was a beautiful summer evening full of tourists, vendors and ghost people. There was so much history Summer could hardly stand it. She was obsessed with history, especially the Revolutionary and Civil Wars. While passing by the Dobbin House, Summer stopped to read the sign posted near the sidewalk. The Dobbin House had been there since the Revolutionary War. It was built in 1776 by the Reverend Alexander Dobbin. During the 1850's to 1860's the Underground Railroad was in full force, hiding runaway slaves heading to freedom up North. The Dobbin House was used as a station for the Underground Railroad.

After the Battle of Gettysburg ended and the Union and Confederate armies left the small historical town of Gettysburg, the Dobbin House was also used as a Civil War hospital to both wounded and dying soldiers, regardless of the color of their uniform as both the North and South were attended to.

It was amazing how so much history could be preserved. George Washington was Summer Ray's hero. She once heard that he drank at the Dobbin House and almost stopped in at the tavern, just to get a drink, for George of course. But Summer Ray didn't drink. She had enough trouble with her brain without adding alcohol to it.

An excited Summer exclaimed to Kat, "So many shops!"

A claustrophobic Kat said back to Summer, "So many people!"

Saturday evening in Gettysburg, as usual, was full of people from all walks of life. Rich and poor, young and old, single and married, bikers and geeks − Gettysburg was no respecter of persons. The disembodied spirits and other principalities watching closely weren't either.

237

There were usually midnight séances either at the Jennie Wade House or near the Farnsworth House, with the clairvoyants and crowds of curious and sometimes serious onlookers hoping to speak to a dead soldier and orphan, or some other spirit of times past. Those activities always made the slithering, foul and loathsome disembodied demons happy.

But darkness would rather spend its energies seeking revenge on the humans that served the Lamb. The Underworld despised those kinds of "parasites," as they called them. Yet, where God's kids were, there were also Angels of every shape and size as well, watching out for the saints of God and doing battle in the world unseen on their behalf. In fact, it was an Angel of Destiny that led Summer to the only store she walked into her first night back in Gettysburg.

As she and Kat walked down Steinwehr Avenue, they passed by many vendors trying to peddle their wares and offering ghost tours. Across the street at a local restaurant and tavern, people were eating, drinking and enjoying the outside summer air.

Kat asked Summer, "Are you hungry? Do you want to go over there to O'Rorke's?"

Kat jokingly continued, "Look, we can even sit outside and watch the tourists go by."

Summer needed to put her two cents in, "Isn't that what we are, Kat?"

"Well being an historian, you have the excuse of working and I.....Well, I am your Jiminy Cricket. I HAVE to be here to keep you out of trouble. So, technically, no we are not tourists." Kat said as she and Summer both started to laugh.

As Summer's eyes were focused down the street instead of across it, she nearly tripped over the artist sitting on the sidewalk.

Summer was very apologetic, "Oh, I am sorry. Wow! These are amazing." Summer said, almost shell shocked as she looked at the amazing artwork.

The artist asked them, "Would you ladies care to have your picture drawn?"

Summer looked down at the clothes she had on and said, "What? In this outfit? Are you kidding me? I don't think so."

Summer wasn't about to have her picture drawn without her hairbrush close at hand, or an outfit that had at least some sex appeal to it.

Summer then politely told him, "I am Summer Ray, and this is Kat. It is nice to meet you."

The artist grinned, "Hi! I am Wilbur."

Summer stated, "Thanks Wilbur. But no picture today."

The white hair, white beard artist asked in a deep husky voice, "So, what brings you ladies to Gettysburg?"

Kat told him, "Oh, Summer is here looking for a ghost."

Summer looked at her and said, "Good one!"

Wilbur replied with a wide grin on his face, "Oh, don't worry. A lot of people around here are looking for ghosts. It is the ones that actually find them that you have to watch out for."

A curious Summer asked, "And why is that?"

Adding more fuel to the fire he answered, "Ghosts tend to follow and attach themselves to the selected few who can interact with them. Ghosts are known to follow those people home."

"Are you trying to scare me?" Summer inquired.

"Me, ahhhh no. I am a good guy. Now why would I want to do that? Just make sure you keep the lights on at home tonight. You know, just in case," an ornery Wilbur said as he was beginning to crack up.

"And oh, you better get back here all prettied up for a portrait soon," he told Summer Ray.

"Yes Sir!" Summer said as she bent down to hug him.

Kat told him, "It was great meeting you."

Further on down Steinwehr Avenue, Summer's attention was abruptly fixated on a store sign. Summer was spellbound and decided to continue on. She was being led by a magnetic pull down the street. In the distance, Summer saw what appeared to be a radiance of energy flickering from a sign post, hanging outside one of the shops. The sign was surrounded by Light. But not light from the street light or lights from the shop. The strange phenomenon caused Summer to feel as if whatever was inside was calling to her. It was a premonition of some sort. For a split second, Summer thought she saw a person welcoming her into the store.

241

Another vision perhaps, Summer wasn't sure. She just knew the heavenly glow had caught enough of her attention that she wasn't about to walk on by without a look inside to see whatever or whomever it was that was reaching out to her. Summer was much too curious and inquisitive and Nathaniel, the Angel of Destiny, knew it!

The Threshold of Destiny

It was a shop like most other shops in Gettysburg. It was full of Civil War memorabilia — flags, miniatures, books, and other items pertaining to war. But this store was the one. The one for what, Summer did not know. Perhaps she would find information on the General.

Summer told Kat, "I am going in to look around."

Kat informed her friend, pointing to a ladies costume shop, "Okay! I will be there in a minute. I want to look at some of those dresses."

As Summer Ray opened the door, she literally tripped on the front step and almost fell down completely into the foyer.

"Now that's an entrance!" Summer thought. "Thank God, no one saw me," she said as she composed herself.

When Summer turned and took the next step into the store, it was almost as if time stood still, or perhaps it had finally started. Summer couldn't tell. But it was like walking through a portal, crossing over the threshold of destiny. Still oblivious to what was happening she looked up and saw him. He was standing behind the counter smiling at her or laughing at her. Summer had hoped it wasn't the latter of the two. When her heart started racing, she knew she had to force her body to budge or stand there, a grown woman, looking like a blushing teenaged girl. Luckily, Summer managed to move passed the counter without embarrassing herself further. She realized he had to have seen her trip into the store and all she wanted to know was if he was single or married. Isn't it mystifying, this thing called love? A supernatural attraction had hit her right between the eyes.

243

As Summer was consumed by a divine connection with the man behind the counter, she automatically forgot about searching for the General. Luckily, Kat showed up and almost ran into her and they both went looking around the store. Summer was in history heaven. Her ex-husband hated history. It was never a good thing to discuss with him. When Summer wanted to watch something about history on TV, it was always an argument. Summer never connected with Tommy and what she thought was being in love, was nothing more than just plain and simple infatuation. Summer kept wondering about the man behind the counter.

In her own mind she said, "Well, if he noticed me, he will come looking for me."

Summer Ray did not go looking for a man and certainly would not be caught dead with a married one! Yet to her happy surprise, the man behind the counter followed her to the back room. He stood behind her with a clip board in his hand, to *appear* as if he was working. She didn't even notice he was there until she turned to look at another shelf and almost toppled over him.

244

"Being the godly woman that I am, I should have fallen into him." Summer laughed quietly to herself! "Come on Summer. You are a mature woman of God. Say something."

The only thing she could come up with at the present moment was, "Hi! I am Summer Ray. I am an author."

A puzzled Sam asked, "I am Sam and really? What kind of an author?"

A smitten Summer Ray replied, "I don't know. How many kinds are there?"

The man who only introduced himself to her as "Sam," looked at Summer Ray rather puzzled. Summer did not quite fit the normal historian authors that Sam was accustomed to. Quite possibly because she was a woman in Gettysburg who wrote about history!

Summer marched to the beat of her own drum. Never one to follow the crowd, she was considered the "rebellious type." It was part of the reason she had so much trouble in church. Someone was always trying to "reform her." Yeah, like that always went over well with her. The more they tried to "reform her" the more rebellious she became. Summer did not like being told what to do and usually did the opposite. One time she was told it wasn't "godly" to get a tattoo.

A disgruntled Summer asked some of the members of the congregation, "Who are you, my mother?"

So, the very next day, she went and got one. Or like the time when it was told in church by a visiting preacher how some people wear the kind of clothes that they do. You know the ones with "holes in their jeans." Summer did not waste time. She looked down at the hole in one of the knees of her jeans, and right there in front of everybody, stood up and ripped the hole even bigger! The pastor saw what she had done and chuckled. While some of the older religious folks gasped. The pastor knew Summer did not take anyone's religious crap! And he never tried to tell her otherwise.

Still, someone was always trying to cast a non-existent demon out of her. But like the wind, she just couldn't be tamed! She wasn't much for religion. In fact, she hated it. Jesus was never a religious man. He was in a relationship with His Father and that was what true

Christianity was really about. Yet religion had somehow demonically infiltrated itself in such a way it was now more important than the relationship. Summer never pretended to be one of those holy rollers. She just loved God and trusted in Him enough to tell her if He had a problem with the way she dressed.

Sam made it look like he was working, but Summer knew he was just checking her out. That made the butterflies in her stomach flutter even stronger. So much so, she was thankful that Kat interrupted them and asked, "Do you want to do the Orphanage tour or the Jennie Wade tour? Never-mind, I can read your mind. You really want to do the Jennie Wade tour."

Sam chimed in, "A ghost tour? So you are one of those kinds of people."

Summer defiantly asked, "What kind of people?"

Sam replied, "A ghost kind."

Summer inquired, "Is that a problem?"

"Around here? Definitely! But take my card anyway. You know, should you decide to cross over to the non-ghost people side of town." Sam said with a wink and a smile.

As she started walking toward the front door, Summer turned to look at him one more time. Something surreal had suddenly washed over her.

Kat thinking her best friend was in la la land, grabbed her arm and said, "Come on Princess, let's get going."

CHAPTER TWELVE

The Farnsworth House

Neither Kat nor Summer Ray had any idea of the hideous, black scaled, creature following them at close range whose name was Bajub, a hindering wicked spirit from the Underworld. Once the dark powers saw the Angel, Nathanial in motion, Bajub was ordered by his ruler, Woeburn to follow Summer and Kathryn. It was Bajub who tripped Summer as she walked into the store. The Angel, Nathanial had to call for the warrior Angel, Sostar, for support. As soon as the dark spirit saw the great warrior Angel, he knew he was no match for him. So, he contorted his scales, jeered at Sostar and flew off to the Jennie Wade house, leaving in his wake a trail of gray smoke that reeked of mold.

Once at the Jennie Wade house, the hindering wicked spirit, Bajub, and Sanbel, a demon of confusion, were joined by their ruler, Woeburn, who spoke in a gravelly hoarse voice, "We will enlist the help of the spirit of Rosa Carmichael. She has informed me the General has finally found his Summer Ray and will try to help her remember her promise. Sanbel, make sure those two women do not go on a tour of this house!"

Woeburn demanded referring to the Jennie Wade house and continued, "Confuse their path and make sure they are on the Orphanage tour instead."

The inferior demon bowed to his ruler and said, "Yes, my Lord." Sanbel then flew off as commanded, to channel the steps of Summer and Kat to the Orphanage tour.

For about an hour, Summer and her best friend walked to three different places looking to get tickets for the Jennie Wade tour. They seemed to be walking in circles when an obviously frustrated and highly annoyed Kathryn Black asked Summer, "What is going on?"

One store would send them to another store. And the store they were sent to then sent them somewhere else. Finally, thirsty and very hungry, they stopped at the Farnsworth House. A man appearing to be in his late twenties and dressed in Civil War attire as a Confederate, introduced himself as "John" and said that he would be their waiter for the evening. Thank God for Kat's ability for small talk as Summer didn't like to talk. It was part of her injury. She loved to write and text. Oh thank God for texting or she would surely be lost.

But there was something uniquely special about John. He politely asked, "Can I start you ladies off with some drinks?"

Summer replied, "I will have a coke please."

"Iced Tea – unsweetened," was Kat's response.

John happily responded, "Sure thing, I will be right back."

Kat asked her friend, "What is that look on your face. You like him, don't you?"

Summer, trying to act coy replied, "What look and like who?"

Kat said with a smile, "Sam, Summer Ray, Sam."

"Did you see those eyes?" Summer said not really asking a question.

Kat brought Summer back to the real reason why they were in Gettysburg when she asked, "So, does this mean we can forget about looking for your ghost?"

Summer informed her friend, "He isn't MY ghost, and no!"

Just then, John came back with their drinks.

Kat started the introductions to their waiter, John, "This is Summer Ray. She is an author in town looking for a ghost."

An embarrassed Summer responded, "Why do you always tell people that? Perfect strangers do not need to know I am an author. They certainly don't need to know I am looking for a ghost either! They will think I'm crazy."

John replied to Summer in a very sympathetic tone, "Actually, around here, if you aren't looking for a ghost you *ARE* considered crazy."

A confused Summer advised the waiter, "That's not what the bookstore guy just told us."

John tried the best he could to explain, "That's because the historians don't like the ghost people and the ghost people, most of them, don't like the historians."

Kat took over the conversation and said, "We better order our food Summer Ray. We don't have much time and John here doesn't need to get in trouble for fraternizing with the guests."

Summer spoke up first, "Okay, I will have the meatloaf, mashed potatoes and green beans. Oh, and rolls with lots and lots of butter please."

"And I'll have the house salad with ranch dressing," was all that Kat ordered.

A perturbed Summer asked, "A salad, are you freakin kidding me? Seriously, is that is ALL you are ordering?"

"We both know as soon as John brings out your food, you are going to give me half of it." Kat shot back at Summer. A now laughing John said, "I will be back with your order shortly."

"Wow! Look at the time! I better go and get our tickets for the Jennie Wade House, right?" Kat asked while standing up from the booth.

Summer answered, "Yes, for the 100th time, but thank you." A confused Kat asked, "For what?"

"For thinking I am crazy and for standing by me anyway. Real friends are hard to find." Summer told her.

"Okay, enough already. You are starting to make me nauseous." Kat said as she left to go get tickets for the Jennie Wade tour.

Not hearing from Billy all day, Summer reached in her purse to retrieve her cell phone to call him. When he didn't answer, a worried Summer put her head down.

A concerned John asked, "What's wrong?"

An anxious Summer replied, "Oh, I just tried to call my son. He is on a camping trip and didn't answer his cell phone."

John, as he tried to comfort Summer said, "He is probably just out of service area. I am sure he is fine."

"So, you must be a dad yourself. How many kids do you have?" Summer asked him.

John proudly answered, "I have a daughter named Kendall and a son named Aydien."

Not seeing a wedding ring on his left hand, Summer asked, "Are you married?"

John replied, "Nope, not anymore, but my kids are with me."

Summer said with a smile, "Wow, good for you. You sound like a very proud dad."

Summer then asked, "So, is this all you do?"

John answered back with, "No! This is my night job. I am a Soccer Coach by day."

Summer's eyes lit up like a Christmas tree as she said, "Really, I am a Figure Skating Coach."

On that note, Summer and John instantly formed a bond and they both knew it. Just then Kat returned with their tickets.

Summer blurted out, "Wow! You look frazzled. What the hell happened to you?"

"I had to go to three other different stores to get the tickets." Kat said as she sat down to a half a plate of meatloaf, mashed potatoes, green beans and HER salad.

"I brought out an extra plate, just in case you were right." John said to Kat and continued, "Enjoy your meal."

Once the ladies finished eating, they said their goodbyes to John and told him they would be back. John wanted a copy of Summer Ray's book " *The Blessings of Liberty*"[6] and the two of them exchanged phone numbers. John eventually became "Joe" to them, as "only my friends called me Joe."

255

Witchy Rosa

When Kat and Summer arrived at the Jennie Wade parking lot, the tour guides were already accepting tickets from people waiting for a tour. As Summer was listening to the guides, she noticed they were talking about orphans and not Jennie Wade. Summer turned to her friend and asked her what tickets she bought.

Kat told Summer, "Jennie Wade, why?"

By the sound of Kat's voice, Summer was actually afraid to tell her it was not the Jennie Wade tour. As if reading Summer's mind, Kat did not waste another second. She went to one of the tour guides and demanded to know what tour they were about to go on. When the tour guide politely informed her it was the Orphanage tour and not the Jennie Wade tour, Kat proceeded to tell this poor innocent guide, all about her troubles trying to get the right tour.

Summer interrupted. It was more trouble to try to get a refund and they decided it was just best to take the Orphanage tour and wait on the Jennie Wade tour. Neither one of them suspected the actual *real* trouble was caused by Sanbel, a demon of confusion. Which in turn

— the SPIRIT was actually using for *HIS* purpose! The SPIRIT had plans for the evil Witchy Rosa Carmichael. The dark powers always think they can pull the rug over the SPIRIT'S eyes. But when He turns things around to work *HIS* plan and purpose, dejected principalities and demons tend to whimper and whine like little babies because they have to answer to their Master...the Devil!

The nice female tour guide was incredibly theatrical and informative. The orphanage was established right after the Civil War in 1866. At first, the orphanage was run by a woman who actually cared for the orphans, Mrs. Philanda Humiston. Her husband, Sergeant Amos Humiston was killed in the Battle of Gettysburg. His body was found near the railroad tracks on the other side of town, near present day Stratton Street by the fire department. Sergeant Humiston could not be identified by the Confederates who found him. Sadly, but thankfully, gripped in his dead hand was a picture of his three children. One can only imagine how his final moments were spent on this Earth, as he laid there, embracing his children for one last time. It brings tears to even the hardest of hearts. When a newspaper article

257

with the picture of his three children reached Mrs. Humiston, who, at the time, was residing in New York, she immediately identified the children as hers and was also able to identify the remains of her dead husband – no longer an "Unknown."

Three years later, a wicked madwoman by the name of Rosa J. Carmichael took over as "Head Mistress." Rosa tortured the orphans. Some of the Gettysburg townspeople had witnessed the little orphan spirits running around The Soldiers Museum or across the street at Cemetery Hill. Maybe those spirit orphans just wanted to have a real childhood, like any other child, where they could run, jump, laugh and play. A childhood where love, adoration and tender care was not demonically stolen from them. So, who is to say that those who saw them in present day did or did not see them?

The tour group was taken to the cellar of the orphanage, commonly known as "the dungeon." This is where Rosa used to chain and beat the orphan boys. The guide told the group of the many ghost sightings of the orphans looking for love in the eyes of some of the tourists. It was suggested to those who had cameras, "To take as many pictures as possible."

There were many pictures on the cellar walls of what appeared to be actual ghosts.

"This is getting a little creepy!" Summer thought.

Little did Summer and Kat know, it was told to the General McDaniels beforehand what Rosa was up to by some of his Unknowns. They were scouting the area when they came across Rosa out in the streets, hovering around the ladies. When the General arrived at the front of the orphanage, he noticed the dark beings also watching nearby. They were allowing Rosa to do their dirty work.

General McDaniels asked himself, "What dirty work and why to these two women?"

The General then ordered Lt. Colonel George Jameson, "Stay here, outside the orphanage and inform me at once if Woeburn is spotted."

The Lt. Colonel saluted his General and replied, "Yes Sir." He then positioned himself at his post keeping a watchful eye out for that hideous Woeburn.

Rosa was way too curious about the General's interest in Summer and wanted to cause her as much trouble as possible. The General had a special eye for Summer and the Unknowns were strictly warned not to haunt or harass her. When it was told to the General what Rosa was doing, the General raced to the orphanage, on Buttercup.

Summer had already let everyone know her opinions of Rosa. While standing in the midst of the tour group she ominously said out loud, "I'd like to knock her teeth down her throat."

It was an outburst that even surprised Summer, let alone everyone else in the tour. But even then Summer knew Rosa was a witch. Remember, it takes a witch to know a witch and part of Summer's dark past was in witchcraft! Even though she knew she couldn't console any of the orphan boys who were once tortured by that madwoman, she, at the very least, wished she could have tortured Rosa. So much for being a "good Christian."

Summer and Kat followed the group to the very small cubby hole that had a 5' ceiling and dirt as the floor.

Not many people in the tour wanted to actually crawl inside it to take a look, but Summer did not mind. She needed to see for herself if there were any *real* ghosts, and maybe the General had a soft spot for damsels in distress. As Summer crawled into the cubby hole where there were toys left for the orphans, she could not imagine how anyone could be so inhumane as to harm those boys, as this woman once had.

It was at that point Summer Ray once again, voiced her opinion. "That piece of crap Rosa! I would like to see someone chain, beat and torture her!"

The General was in earshot of what Summer had just said and asked himself, "Does this woman ever shut up?"

All Summer could think about at that moment were those kids. As if the war itself wasn't enough of a heartache for them, these were children who lost their fathers. Many lost their mothers either due to illness, or because of the war they just could not afford to raise their children. Imagine being chained to a cellar wall for days without food or water, being beaten by the older boys. Imagine at the tender age of five years old, being locked outside in the freezing cold in an outhouse, there again without food and water. The sheer terror these children suffered, there were simply no words to describe it.

All Summer knew is that she wished she could do to Rosa what Rosa had done to those kids, and she had no problem expressing it. Summer didn't fear ghosts! She just didn't know if they actually existed. Summer knew the darkness existed as many a times she was faced with it. But, the stronger she grew in Spiritual Warfare, the less the darkness exposed itself to her, for fear of being sent to the abyss.

Rosa did not see the General standing behind her. Summer did not see Rosa on top of her with Rosa's hands around her neck. All Summer knew, within a few short seconds, her heart was pounding in her chest and she became very hot and weak. For a split second she felt trapped, as she could not breathe nor swallow. As panic set in, Summer tried to crawl back out of the cubby hole but couldn't. She was losing consciousness as she was drifting into a trance or into a coma of some sort. She knew where she was, she just couldn't speak or move.

As Rosa began to strangle Summer, the General immediately pierced Rosa with his sword. Surrounded by orbs and other imps, the General didn't have time to call for his Unknowns. So, with his sword, he hit the metal pipes over top of Kat's head, hoping the noise would get her attention. Summer needed to be pulled out of the cubby hole and fast, or quite possibly she would be strangled to death by Rosa.

In the spirit world you could hear Rosa grunt out in pain as the sword perforated into her and she said to the General, "You think you can stop me, do you?"

Just then Rosa called for the demons of "Sorcery" and "Witchcraft."

Upon hearing the noise above her head, shocking her to the point she wanted to run out of the cellar, Kat turned and saw Summer in a trance like state and it freaked her out even more. All at once, the Angel, Lancelot, latched onto Summer Ray and pulled her out of the cubby hole so forcefully, it knocked both her and Kat down. All that could be seen were shimmering traces of angelic gold dust invading the darkness of the cellar, and what appeared to be the outline of giant white wings glistening like diamonds. This in fact, forced Summer to come to, and once again she was brought back from going under to the other side.

Barely able to stand up, Summer began to shake off the remnants of dirt, of what had just happened to her. All of the sudden, that feeling of suffocation left and her mind regained itself and she was finally able to speak. Though the General wished at times she wouldn't, it was no secret how outspoken Summer was.

Kat asked her friend, "Are you okay? What the hell happened to you?"

A disoriented Summer whispered back, "I don't know. But thank you for pulling me out."

Kat informed her friend, "I didn't pull you out."

Summer replied, "What do you mean you didn't pull me out? You were the only one standing by the cubby hole."

"Summer, I didn't pull you out." Kat's tone of voice changed to the point Summer believed her.

"If you didn't pull me out, then who did?" Summer asked as others in the tour group rushed to help Summer and Kat get back up to their feet.

Though unbearably cramped, it was nice that others offered their assistance. It was at that time that the tour guide summoned everyone back outside, fully aware of what was going on. She too was once faced with a troublesome Witchy Rosa.

Summer didn't tell anyone of what she had just experienced. She just chalked it up to being claustrophobic. When someone asked the tour guide why she wouldn't go near the cubby hole or crawl space, she informed them that she wouldn't tell anyone while there were children still in their group, as she didn't want to "scare them." Those who wanted to know, she would tell them after the tour.

Once back outside the orphanage, the General summoned his scouts and told them not to leave Summer or her friend. As promised, after the tour, the guide told those with inquiring minds the real reason she refused to go back into the cubby hole or crawl space at the orphanage. She proceeded to tell them the same exact experience she herself suffered, much like the one that Summer just had. When Summer heard the guide tell the rest of the group how she couldn't breathe and how her heart started pounding in her chest, Summer realized that Rosa was the one who had attacked her, and that it wasn't just a case of claustrophobia.

Summer asked herself, "A ghost obviously cannot kill a human being or can it?"

Seeing how Summer felt herself going into a coma like state and she couldn't even bring herself to say the word "Jesus," it almost felt like death was wrapped around her neck. This was no ordinary attack. Why? What did Summer have to do with Rosa? Did Rosa hear what Summer said about her? Although that didn't change what Summer thought about Rosa, it certainly unnerved her that she was attacked by that depraved witch.

Sostar and Rory took out the demon spirits of Sorcery and Witchcraft and sent them back to their prince, Woeburn, at Devil's Den. If Summer Ray was starting to come apart at the seams, it didn't show to the general public. But inwardly, she was starting to find some very dangerous cracks in her armor. She was starting to weaken and Discourage, another principality, had recognized it.

With the tour over and no sign of the General, a bummed Summer and an exhausted Kathryn went back to the Travelodge only a few blocks away. Neither Summer nor Kat suspected what just emerged right around them at the orphanage. Summer was there to find the General, not knowing the General once again had helped save her life.

The Pieces

Though documented, no one in current day actuality will ever understand fully what the townspeople of Gettysburg suffered during the aftermath of the battle fought there. As blood was spilled on every street corner, no one back then really understood the severity of contaminated blood. Now a day's, if you happen to prick your finger on something, people panic. The fact that so much of Gettysburg has been preserved since the war is a phenomenon in and of itself.

No wonder so many people flock to it year after year, and why the town is full of historians, ghost people, re-enactors, soldiers, and tourists. Yet it is also full of witches, warlocks, demons, devils, orbs, imps and Angels! And somewhere out in those fields, buried beneath the soil, are the remains of some fallen Union or Confederate soldier that only if God so chooses, will ever be found. Like the remains of a New York soldier who died at Antietam and was recently unearthed.

The Confederate Army did not consider themselves to be United States soldiers. After the war however, though forced, they once again were re-united with the rest of the country. The manager at the Soldiers National Museum told those in Summer's ghost tour group about a disgruntled spirit named William who hangs out and guards Devil's Den. A Confederate soldier, wearing no shoes, with bullet holes throughout his uniform, William would never admit to such an atrocity as the Confederates now being United States soldiers.

The certainty about Gettysburg is that things don't have to make sense to be true. Luckily, Kat and Summer hadn't heard much about the Travelodge being haunted, something Kat was thankful for. Summer pondered all that had been happening and like a good detective, kept trying to put all the pieces together to make some sense out of it all. But, without the proper information, there were just too many gaps to form a conclusion. Summer would just have to wait. Tomorrow was another day, with another tour, if one was necessary.

As Kat and Summer sat outside on the balcony in the night air, the stars were shining high above them and they began to reminisce about their college years together. Kat was with Summer when she visited the Tops while Summer was doing research for her college thesis, as she is the one who took her off the hill and drove her straight to the Gettysburg Hospital. Kat never brought it up, as Summer couldn't remember it. She always felt that Summer would not miss what she could not remember. But little did she know, Kat contained some of the missing pieces to Summer's past and her troubled present. As Summer began rubbing her palm, Kat noticed Summer's distant expression, as if she were in another place trying to remember something.

Kat spoke up, "What is it Summer? Ever since Gettysburg came back to life in you, you have been a million miles away."

A puzzled Summer asked, "What do you mean came back to life in me? Have we done this before?"

Not waiting for an answer, Summer continued speaking, "I feel as if I *HAVE* been here before. You know like from another time and not just our time – like I get the feeling while I am here in Gettysburg that I am part of its history somehow. I know that sounds crazy. But I have dreams of rocks, blood and snow. I have dreams of eyes and of death. It's all so confusing."

Kat did not understand the time Summer was referring to was the actual Gettysburg battle in 1863 as she said, "You were here before Summer. Don't you...No! I guess you don't remember. When we were in college, you wrote your college thesis on the Battle of Gettysburg. We drove to Little and Big Round Tops in the dead of winter. You were determined to write your paper there and your dad let us use his four-wheel drive! Do you remember any of that Summer?"

As soon as Summer tried to remember "any of that," as usual, a sharp pain shot across the back of her skull.

Kat seeing the pain in Summer's eyes continued, "Okay Summer Ray, enough down memory lane. You have had way too many jolts to your brain as it is tonight. I don't want you going into a seizure because of another blow to your head. Cuz quite frankly, that would suck more for me than for you."

Summer vainly replied, "Okay."

But, at least it did put Summer's mind at some ease. She wasn't as crazy as she was beginning to think, and if he existed, she knew exactly where to find the elusive General McDaniels.

The Right Kind of Help

Meanwhile, back at Seminary Ridge, Captain Talhelm, was giving orders to his heavenly host.

Jasper, an impulsive, yet ruthless warrior Angel, spoke up and asked his Captain, "Why can't we do more for Summer. I mean right now! She doesn't know what the darkness is planning against her."

As he placed his right hand on Jasper's left shoulder, a patient Captain Talhelm responded, "In time, my friend in time. She will come to a place where what she has learned about the Lord and His faithfulness, and He will come to her rescue. There are some things that humans must endure for the sake of a deeper and closer walk with the Lord. If Summer loses her faith, we cannot help her to find it. Angels are not redeemed like humans are. If they fall away from the Father, Son and the Holy Spirit, all we can do is sit back and watch them go in great sadness.

We rejoice when they receive salvation, and are sad when they walk away from it. We must obey the *SPIRIT* no matter how much we want to rush in to help her. But, should the *SPIRIT* summon us to her side, you can be sure we will be there. Her prayers are being offered up as soon as they leave her mouth. But she cannot withstand this kind of evil alone. She must have help, the right kind of help and that is prayer support. If the right kind of prayer support is offered, we are here to give her that right kind of help. I cannot give the order to fight until the *SPIRIT* gives it to me. So, rest for now, my young friend, just rest. I sense the battle will increase. I feel the darkness growing stronger, and soon enough He will summon us!"

CHAPTER THIRTEEN

The Meeting

At dawn, Summer told her friend she was going out for a morning walk and would be back for breakfast in about an hour. Kat was thankful she wasn't asked to go with her as she just wanted to sleep in. Luckily, she didn't ask Summer any questions as "going out for a morning walk" was another one of those "sort of true" statements.

As Summer was walking toward her car, looking over toward Baltimore and Steinwehr Avenues, she thought, "Wow! The town of Gettysburg on a Sunday morning really is like a ghost town."

But she was on a mission to find this ghostly General Michael Moses McDaniels. Summer drove as fast as she could to the Tops without getting a ticket for speeding. Seeing how most of the speed limit in Gettysburg is 25 to 35mph, that was especially hard to do. Although, she wanted to drive at warped speed, she still had to obey the law.

When she got to the bottom of Big Round Top, she had this overwhelming feeling as if she had been there before, like Deja` Vu. But she didn't have time to analyze it. She pulled her silver Honda Civic over to the side, shut it off, jumped out of her vehicle and tried the best she could to run up the hill. Summer didn't notice the US Confederate and Union Unknown Soldiers watching her from a distance, nor the General at the top! She tripped a few times, slid back down and tried to run up the hill again. Never mind the cement stairs that were visible nearby, and the clear foot path to walk up the hill. She was so angry at the General she didn't care how foolish she looked.

Once she reached the top, she yelled at the top of her lungs, "General Michael Moses McDaniels, are you here?"

She waited for an answer without a reply.

Summer looked around Big Round Top with the sunrays peeking through the tall trees and yelled again, "General Michael Moses McDaniels, are you here?"

The Unknowns were starting to get restless and on edge. So much so, they began to move about in the midst of the trees. The hair on Summer's neck began to stand up and chills ran down the back of her spine as shadowy phantoms in blue and gray vaguely began to emerge. She could see the trees begin to sway back and forth. As the wind was rustling through the leaves, Summer's long hair began to fly about in her face.

Frozen with fear at the possible fact that all this ghost stuff was actually true, a brave Summer put her free-flowing hair back behind her ears and with her hands firmly planted on her hips, she yelled out again, "General Michael Moses McDaniels, are you here? I am not leaving until you answer me! Are you here?"

Just then, from behind her, down the hill a little ways, she heard the words that would forever change her life, "Well, yes Ma'am...I am!"

When Summer Ray heard them, not knowing what she was about to see, and with her heart pounding in her chest, taking an act of resolute courage, she slowly turned around to face him. When she finally saw him, she almost fainted at the sight of him. He wore the same uniform he had on in her dream a few nights before. He was sinfully handsome, but she didn't have time to think about that at the moment.

Almost paralyzed from shock and unable to take a step forward, Summer demanded to know and asked the General, "Why are you haunting me?"

The General gazed at Summer, hating her and loving her all at the same time. He had so many mixed emotions about this wild woman standing before him. After all, she didn't take into account that she was yelling at a ghost. As Summer's body finally allowed her to advance forward so that she could approach the General, the Unknowns standing closest to her restrained her. This was their General and it was their duty to protect him. At that moment Summer felt arms holding her own and when she looked to see whose they were she almost fainted, again!

Summer saw the hands that restrained her, hands that were bloodstained, dusty and strong. When she looked up at their faces, she gasped in horror as she saw none. She then looked around the hill and saw thousands of Unknowns in their tattered Union or Confederate uniforms, blood stained bodies without faces. They had no eyes, no ears, no nose or mouth. Only their forehead could be seen that were either marked with the words "US Unknown" or a black number etched there, like the graves marked at The Gettysburg National Cemetery. When Summer saw that they were mostly teenaged boys and young men, she broke down in tears as she thought of her own son Billy.

Imagine the petrified astonishment at seeing these soldiers. As a parent, Summer could not imagine what their mothers and fathers must have gone through. They had watched their loving sons go off to war. When the war was over, their grief-stricken parents could never find closure. The mangled bodies of their dead sons could not be identified and their sons could not be given a proper burial. As the parents waited for the list of those killed, missing or wounded, there was no word about what the fate of their sons would be. How unimaginably horrifying!

The General nodded to the soldiers who held her to let her go. The General stepped back as Summer began to walk in the midst of the Unknowns, who could be seen in human form, but only on Big Round Top.

279

With the palm of her right hand, she began to touch what should have been the faces of those United States Unknown soldiers. Though she had no feeling in her hands, touching them gave her a sense of connection. Summer knew, had the Union lost the war, she might possibly had never been born. She didn't know whether to thank the Union Unknowns or not, as they were standing side by side with the Confederate Unknowns.

The General seeing her bewilderment told her, "We may have died as enemies, but we were resurrected as brothers."

Summer was astounded at the amount of suffering these soldiers had had to endure, in a war that never should have happened. The fact that most of them were so young was a sadness Summer Ray could hardly bear. With tears streaming down her face, she went to the General and pushed him, once again demanding to know what promise he was talking about. Getting pushed was just about as much as the General could stand. He grabbed Summer Ray's right hand and turned it over so he could see the scars on her palm. As Summer Ray screamed out in pain, the General was beside himself with fury — fury at her not remembering her promise — fury at his ex-wife's betrayal — fury at the war which caused so much horror and bloodshed.

Summer screamed at the General, "Let go of me!"

The General angrily shouted back at her, "These scars, where did they come from?"

Summer answered, "I don't know where they came from. Let go of my hand. You are hurting me!"

Furious, the General howled, "What do you mean you do not know. They are on *YOUR* hand!"

The General had simply lost all patience with this woman, and the past that Summer had forgotten was about to abruptly be brought back.

"Ten years ago, you were on this hill. There was snow and ice on the ground. The Lt. Colonel Jameson and I watched you as you tripped. We saw you grab *THAT* thorn bush right over there to stop yourself from falling down the hill. You sliced open your hand and when you looked down at the snow, you saw blood, your own blood. It was then you realized that the blood of others who died in the Battle of Gettysburg was still here, crying out for justice. When your friend yelled out for you and you did not answer, she climbed up the hill to get you. By the time she reached you, I covered your hand in snow to stop you from bleeding to death, and stood you up back on your feet. When your friend started to walk you back down the hill, you turned to me and said, 'Thank you. I will be back and I promise I will do whatever I can to bring you peace.' That was ten years ago and this is the first we have seen you!"

Summer cried out, "I don't know what you are talking about."

The General grabbed Summer again, and this time with anger in his eyes, the likes none of which the Unknowns had ever seen.

One of them courageously spoke up, "General, Sir, perhaps you are being too hard on her!"

The General shot a ghostly look at the brave Union Unknown, then turned back to Summer and said, "What do you mean you do not know what I am talking about? If you were not on this hill ten years ago, then where did these scars come from?"

Summer now close to hysterical shouted, "I told you, I don't know!"

The General snapped back, "You are lying!"

Summer's next words cut the General deep, "And you're just a bitter, angry old spirit who hates women!"

The Unknowns took a few steps backwards and looked at each other, wondering what the General was about to do next. Although they all knew what Summer said was the truth, none of them ever dared to say such a thing to him. After all, they were United States soldiers and knew their place.

Summer didn't give him a second to reply and continued on with her assault, "Yeah! I read all about your wife leaving you for another man. I read how in battle you dropped your guard and how a cannonball exploded right in the middle of your own men!"

The General dropped Summer's hand and started to walk up the hill out of sight. One of Summer Ray's faults was that she just didn't know when to quit. In a haughty and triumphant tone she yelled out, "Walking away is for cowards!"

With one swift movement, General Michael Moses McDaniels pinned Summer Ray between himself and one of the rocks. The General had had enough of her over active and razor-sharp tongue, and he kissed Summer Ray so hard she thought her mouth would fall off.

When an enraged General McDaniels hissed, "Do not ever call me a coward again! If I hate women so much, I would have let Rosa suffocate you when she had her hands wrapped around your neck!" Summer knew she had simply gone too far. She dropped her head because she couldn't bear to look the General in the eyes.

"Who's the coward now?" He asked, then said, "At least I am not a liar."

Summer, in her defense told him, "If I was here ten years ago, I have no memory of it. I was in a car accident. I hit my head and suffered severe brain trauma. Everything before that is wiped out. I have no memory of it. I told you, I didn't know where these scars came from. I was telling you the truth and you didn't believe me!"

Our Suffering

At that point, Summer was crying hysterically. As she became limp in his arms, the General's heart seemed to have started beating again. He had vented his wrath on Summer and he knew it. He also knew she suffered an injury that had quite possibly meant she was telling him the truth. Yes, he was a coward, he thought to himself. He knew he had hurt her, and he just didn't know how to bring himself to apologize. So, he dropped her, and as she fell to the ground, General McDaniels disappeared out of sight. A Confederate and Union Unknown rushed to Summer's side and she cried like she had never cried before. The Unknowns knew that she was bewailing for their suffering as well as her own.

In sobs, and bent over in anguish, she cried out, "I'm sorry. I am so so sorry. Your parents, oh God your families, your beloveds, your friends — they never saw you again!" Summer had no recollection of the time she was on that same hill ten years earlier, in the dead of winter in the ice and snow, and how she was taken back in time to the actual battle itself. All she knew was present day and these brave soldiers with no faces.

A Confederate soldier with the words "US Unknown" etched across his forehead spoke, "Summer Ray!" He said, as he lifted her chin so that her tear stained face could look at him. "We are now United States American Soldiers. That is who we are. Though we will not be remembered for our names, we are remembered for our service and for our sacrifice. Though I fought on the losing side, I fought for what I believed in. I died for what I believed in. It wasn't wrong for me to die for the Cause I gave my all for. You must not allow our suffering to destroy your hope of a better future. All of us, as we stand here before you – we gave our all for our country."

A Union Unknown, with just a number marked across his forehead began to speak, "Slavery was wretched, and President Lincoln stood up for the Union. God made a way through that great leader to begin to dismantle slavery from this great country. He made a way through that great leader to keep this country a united one. Though some of us here fought on opposing sides, we were buried as brothers as Unknowns. It took that great Civil War to make this country what it is today. Had it not been for our suffering and others like us who are

286

named – you and others like you, might not have ever been born. Had it not been for our suffering and others like us who are named, your friend's ancestors, and others like her, might still be bound in the chains of slavery. God made sure the Union won the war so that the scourge of slavery could be destroyed."

"But if you can't leave Gettysburg, how will you ever find peace?" Summer Ray finally spoke in between her tears, feeling as if their peace, and the weight of the world were on her shoulders. "I don't know what promise the General is referring to!" Summer said looking down at the ground. When Summer Ray looked up to ask the Unknowns if they had seen her on Big Round Top before, they had vanished. For whatever reason, it was not time for Summer to remember everything.

Quite possibly added shock would have been too much for her. Rory, her Guardian Angel, dressed in camouflage with a gold sword attached to his belt, standing tall and authoritative on one of the rocks above was there, on Big Round Top, guarding Summer. When

Rory motioned to the Unknowns to disappear, they evaporated into thin air.

Suddenly aware she was left on Big Round Top alone, Summer yelled out, "I wish I could do that!"

Standing up she brushed the dirt off her jeans and wiped the tears out of her eyes. When Rory heard what she had said, off the rock he soared and landed right beside Summer. Though he was invisible to her naked eye, spiritually she could sense that someone was there. Maybe it was the way the sun began to shine through the trees onto the rocks that caused them to dazzle and sparkle, like a sunray beaming off the ocean. Or maybe it was the heavenly gift of serenity that suddenly filled Summer's soul. But when the realization finally struck her that it was only 7:00AM on a Sunday morning and she was a woman alone on Big Round Top, Summer decided it was best to leave Gettysburg.

As a very weary Summer Ray drove her Honda Civic back to the Travelodge, Gristmill, a dark brown, furry wicked scout from the Underworld with long hideous black nails, was indeed pleased with her fatigue! Summer was mentally, physically and emotionally drained, and the vile powers below had every intention of taking advantage of her exhaustion.

Meanwhile, the General, back on Big Round Top, was none too pleased with himself. As he watched Summer Ray fade off into town, he wondered if he would ever see her again. He knew he could not go after her and informed his Unknowns they were going to town at dusk. The Unknowns knew it was going to be a sad night for the townspeople of Gettysburg.

A Union Unknown said, "A sad night indeed!"

Summer Ray went back to the Travelodge, and while packing her bag, she informed Kat that they would, "Grab a bite at McDonald's" and "Get the hell out of Dodge!"

One look at Summer and Kathryn Black was happy to oblige.

CHAPTER FOURTEEN

A Moment of Weakness

The Unknowns hadn't seen their General this incensed in a very long time. He was at war within himself, and from the looks of things, the real Michael Moses McDaniels was losing. They held their peace hoping the General wouldn't cross the line. Although the spirits were allowed to harass and haunt, and although some had even gone so far as to kill a human or to drive them crazy enough they chose to kill themselves, the Unknowns knew they lived under the Stars and Stripes.

The war was over and these brave and valiant soldiers were just waiting for their eternal rest. They knew their General, though ranked as a Colonel during the Civil War, thought he had stayed behind to help his regiment, like any good officer is supposed to do.

But for some reason, there just seemed to be another explanation as to why the Colonel made such an unselfish decision. While, he himself, could have crossed over to the other side, where tranquility and paradise were waiting for him, away from all the horrific reminders of the war that cost him his life, he chose to stay in the torture and torment of his lost soul.

Before the Colonel left to fight in the Civil War, he was married to the love of his life, Lily. After the war they planned to start a family. But before the war was over, Lily ran off with an accountant and divorced Michael Moses McDaniels. Lily told the Colonel she didn't want to have to wait for his companionship. Her reason being, the lonely nights were just too...well you know, lonely! When word reached the Colonel that she had not only left him, but divorced him, it was as if a minie ball had already made its way through his heart. He died even before he was mortally wounded in battle. But he damned himself.

In a split second of time, while musing over the heartache, an artillery shell exploded overheard, not far from the Colonel and his men. All of them, except the Colonel, were instantly killed. The wounds they suffered were so ghastly and so horrific that no one, except for the Colonel and the Lt. Colonel, could be properly identified. The others were listed as "Unknown." He saw

292

the trampled wheat cushioning the lifeless and butchered bodies of his regiment. That sight alone would have been enough to stop the heart of their Colonel, had he not already been mortally wounded and slowly dying himself.

The Colonel never forgave himself for what he presumed to be weakness and carried the burden of his men's deaths to his own. He vowed to stay by their side until they all could find peace for such a dark and tragic loss. Soon after, other Unknowns followed, and then others and others after that, to where they numbered by the thousands of US Unknown soldiers.

There were a great many conflicts still between the Blue and the Gray. It wasn't until Roosevelt's dedication of the Eternal Light Peace Memorial, on July 3, 1938 that the Unknowns were finally able to stand together, not as Union soldiers or Confederate soldiers, but as soldiers of the United States of America. When President Roosevelt gave the signal, the American flag that was draped over the memorial fell into the hands of both a Union and Confederate veteran. A flame was lit on top of the memorial as a signal of eternal peace for all those who fought in Gettysburg, and for the country at large.

Hands Across the Wall

At the 50th reunion of the Anniversary of the Battle of Gettysburg, members of the Philadelphia Brigade Association and Pickett's Division Association met at the "Stone Wall" crossing the dimensions of space and time. As these elderly Union and Confederate veterans, some with canes in their left hand, reached across the wall with their right hand and shook the hands of the men who were once their mortal enemies.

There simply cannot be words to describe the astonishing moment in history that event must have been. It was a sacred and hallowed place where their fellow comrades fell. It was a blessed land where the bravest of all men, the Confederate Soldiers, obeying the commands of their superior officers, stared down the barrels of cannons, as they marched across the open field. These brave men, knowing certain death was upon them, engulfed in the flames of fear, courageously marched forward for their country, marking them for all eternity as true American soldiers.

At the 75th reunion of the Anniversary of the Battle of Gettysburg, the same day Roosevelt dedicated the Eternal Light Peace Memorial, with just a handful of veterans left, the youngest of the veterans of the Union and Confederate Civil War Soldiers was 90 years old. Amazingly enough, the veterans that couldn't walk were carried on stretchers, pushed in wheel chairs, or driven in cars for the parade. These determined and adamant men were not about to miss the anniversary of the battle they fought in seventy-five years before.

This conviction, within the depths of their souls, was not for their own enlistment. It was also for their fellow comrades, since the first shot was fired in 1861. Neither the Union organization, called the "Grand Army of the Republic," nor the Confederate organization, called, the "United Confederate Veterans" stopped attending these reunions until there were no more living veterans on either side.

295

In his spirit form, General Michael Moses McDaniels stood watching, and saluted the remaining veterans as they passed by. All in attendance at this particular parade must have known it was to be the last one of its kind. An era was passing, times were changing, and America was evolving, as technology was rapidly growing. Yet, the Civil War, especially the battle of Gettysburg, even well into the 21st Century, remained branded into the hearts and souls of the living, as well as the dead.

Retribution

The General was, in some opinions of other spirits, "in rare form." He wasn't his usual cautious self. He respected the territories of other disembodies, orbs or what have you, except when Rosa tried to hurt Summer. The General was so displeased with the town of Gettysburg that he managed to snarl the regular route of traffic on Baltimore Street and on several occasions almost caused a few accidents. There was yelling in the

296

streets by angry pedestrians who couldn't cross at the crosswalks. The lights never turned red. They stayed green in every direction. Although the General got a kick out of it, it wasn't enough to appease his wounded ego.

While haunting humans on a ghost tour, he scared the living daylights out of one woman and her husband. They were behind the orphanage near the cemetery when this couple happened to look out to the dark field. The General told a few of his Unknowns to "do it and do it right!" For a split second, five of the Unknowns could be seen, in spirit form, fighting each other. The woman almost passed out and the husband's face was as white as the Unknowns faces were themselves. When the couple shouted to the others in the group what they had seen, the Unknowns as usual, were gone.

Some of the spirits went dashing and soaring through hotels, banging pots and pans, and pulling blankets off of innocent and bewildered patrons. Though not a breezy night in Gettysburg, some of the signs outside were swaying back and forth. One spirit went so far as to spill an entire dinner plate on someone. Then the ghostly foul proceeded to throw several trays of newly washed dinner glasses across the dining room, shattering them into millions of pieces. Luckily, no-one was injured.

Yes! There was a dismal overcast that had settled over the townspeople. But they were used to it. It was the tourists that never could quite come to grips with it all. Children were clinging to their parents, especially on the Orphanage tour. One of the tourists reported hearing the cries of what sounded like little boys. If Rosa acted up again, no one said. She might have been too afraid of the General as she knew he was out wandering the streets.

Hour by hour passed, and the General still did not feel any sense of satisfaction from his exploits. In fact, the more he tried to scare people, the less he felt good about himself. Something that surprised him as normally he took great delight in haunting the humans. Yet, this time it was different. Something inside him though transparent, as a ghost, his conscience was starting to get the better of him. He knew the only remedy for his wounded ego was to apologize to Summer. He had blamed her for his former wife's actions and for his own. Summer was not a scapegoat! The General finally conceded.

298

It was nearing dawn and the General rounded up his Unknowns. Other spirits and orbs stayed where they were, but for his Unknowns, it was back to Big Round Top. The General told his soldiers that he knew he had made a terrible mistake. Although they were happy to hear that, they all wondered if it was too late. Redemption for them, they all knew, might never come. The General was a tortured spirit that he could not seem to forgive others of their wrong doing. Admitting to a mistake was one thing, forgiving a mistake was quite another.

If Union and Confederate veterans could stand with hands across a wall that once shattered their lives with bloodshed, surely this Michael Moses McDaniels could discover some fragment and sense of freedom in the sacrificial acts of those war-torn veterans. Yet, that was not to be. The key to his rest was forgiveness. It wasn't a magic wand that could be waved. It was an attitude of the heart that needed to be understood. If the General and the Unknowns were ever going to find eternal rest and escape the bonds that held them between the now and eternity, General Michael Moses McDaniels needed a

299

miracle, the miracle of Summer Ray Sherwood's memory.

CHAPTER FIFTEEN

Soul Searching

It was Monday morning and the phone rang. A still worn out Summer didn't look at who it was.

She answered, "Hello?"

A jubilant Billy yelled, "Mom, it's me!"

A beaming Summer replied to her son, "Hi, Sweetie. Are you having fun? I tried to call you last night to say, 'Good night,' but your dad didn't answer his cell phone."

Billy responded, "Yeah! There is no service at some look out points," an excited Billy exclaimed, "but we are going canoeing today! I just wanted to call and tell you I love and miss you."

"I love and miss you too, Sweetie. I can't wait for you to come home!" Summer told her son and began to softly cry as she thought of the Unknowns on Big Round Top.

Billy said to his mom, "Aww, Mom! Don't cry!"

Summer lied, "What? I am not crying!"

Billy, knowing the truth, said, "Yes you are, Mom. I know you!"

"Okay, well, I guess you got me there! I am crying because I have the best son any mom could ever ask for!" Summer tried to make her tears sound like happy ones.

"And you're the best mom! Gotta go! Bye." Billy said and hung up the phone before his mom could say "bye" too.

As Summer put her cell phone back on the night stand, she could only thank God that Billy was safe and sound. She thought of the soldiers in Iraq and Afghanistan and became more fervent in her prayers for their safe return. Summer knew how fortunate she was to live in America and was becoming more and more aware as the days wore on. She too was the daughter of a military man. Her dad, John Walter Sherwood, was in the Navy. Summer was also a soldier, but not for America.

Summer was in God's army, and at times felt she might go AWOL. Her disabilities created a weak spot in her armor. She was beginning, for the first time in her life, to feel that she was defenseless, helpless and vulnerable. Summer knew she wasn't any of those things with God in her life, but wasn't it God who allowed her to become those things in the first place with that car accident? She survived, but with missing pieces it seemed like. The thought that Billy wasn't in the car with her gave her the ability to not allow despair to get the better of her. Billy was safe and alive. She couldn't have asked for more.

Summer recovered and had recently found, within the depths of her own heart, a root of bitterness. Underneath that rough and tough exterior of hers, was lies the emptiness of a woman's soul that had yet to find the love she so desperately wanted. The words describing Jennie Wade in Kenneth Neff Hammontree's book "*There Was A Time; A Civil War Romance*,"[12] described exactly how Summer felt at times.

> "*She sometimes felt that real love was something that would happen to someone else, but never her.*"

Maybe Summer's rough and tough exterior was there to hide her true self, like a mask trying to cover something very fragile up. Although Summer was never one for pretense, she certainly did not want anyone to know just how much she wanted to be loved and needed by the right man. Who that was, she couldn't imagine. The only man who took that sinking feeling in her stomach away was that man in her dream, and she didn't even know who he was or if he was even real. However, the General turned out to be real enough alright, and maybe a little too real.

The General may be a ghost, but his words and actions stung deep. It was bad enough to be treated like that by her ex-husband, but by a ghost, too? Summer was beginning to think there was something terribly wrong with her, like she wasn't capable of being loved.

Summer silently asked, "What's wrong with me?"

She just couldn't comprehend as to why love had eluded her to the extent that it had. Real love, that is: the Jennie and Jack kind of love, or the Johnny and June kind of love.

Summer thought to herself, "Their love was a real fairytale kind of love."

The reason fairytales exist is so that people can believe in them. Summer only wanted real love. She only wanted to be with the man that she was created for. The man who would look at her like Adam looked at Eve when he said, "*This is now bone of my bone and flesh of my flesh.*"* Summer wanted nothing more than to find this Adam of hers. Maybe finally admitting that to herself, she could stop pretending and start allowing herself to be vulnerable. Possibly learning how to be vulnerable was precisely the reason why God allowed her car accident. He certainly wasn't the cause of it. Summer was a strong woman, indeed. But maybe that was self-strength and not the God kind of strength. Self-reliance is nothing more than stupid pride, as Summer was starting to understand. It wasn't that Tommy had immediately left her after the car accident, Summer had to admit. Perhaps she had pushed him away. Maybe she didn't like who she had become and she took her pain out on him. Maybe the pain of not being able to ice skate like she used to left her feeling like she wasn't whole.

Tom wasn't God, and he didn't have the ability to give back to her what she had lost. Part of Summer's soul was out on that ice, jumping and spinning. To this day, Summer had not overcome that loss, even with her being a coach. Oftentimes she found herself jealous when she saw another skater doing what she used to be able to do. Maybe it was that jealousy that led to a bitter heart, as one sin begets another sin. All this soul searching and Summer hadn't even climbed out of bed yet.

Summer still pondering thought to herself, "There is no way I could ever go back to Tom. He and I are just not the right match. But, I should stop being so hard on him. Maybe I should finally tell him I am sorry and ask for his forgiveness at how I may have treated him after my accident. Perhaps that will give Billy a better sense that his parents, though not together, at least are not sworn enemies."

Summer was trying to get back to normal, or as normal as humanly possible while having a ghost mad at her. She had to laugh at herself because a few months ago, she didn't even believe in ghosts. But she knew the General had dismissed her as if she were one of his soldiers who had gone AWOL and was being given a dishonorable discharge. She knew it was pointless to try and avenge herself. It was too painful, the look of distrust in his eyes. She just couldn't bear it. But she knew that Gettysburg was part of her life as an author who wrote about it. She had book signings coming up at a few local shops, and she wasn't about to miss those opportunities because of an angry ghost who hated her. Summer knew she had to go back again to Gettysburg!

A Frail Little Human

While musing all of this over, and just talking to the Lord about it, Summer had a vision. Still lying in the comfort of her bed, she saw a witch hovering over little boys sitting on the brick wall at the Jennie Wade house. The witch was none other than the wicked Rosa Carmichael. She held in her hand a wand full of green poison. As these boys were playing and talking to each other, Rosa would tap them on the shoulder with the wand, cursing them and poisoning them for life. When Summer came out of the vision, her spirit rose up in the same kind of anger it had when she was in the cellar at the orphanage.

Summer shouted out loud, "It *REALLY WAS* the spirit of Rosa Carmichael that attacked me. But what is she still doing poisoning little boys?"

No one knows what happened to the human Rosa Carmichael. Once she was banned from Gettysburg for torturing the orphans, she was never heard from again. There is nothing on public record about where she went or how she died. But upon her death, her disembodied, depraved and wicked spirit returned to Gettysburg to carry on its former human's malicious deeds of poison, torture and death.

Summer screamed, "OH MY GOD!" As she jumped out of bed and ran to her dresser, Summer knew she didn't have time to take a shower or to even brush her long hair, so she just put it in a ponytail. Once dressed in blue jeans and a t-shirt, Summer ran to her car and drove the thirty minutes to Gettysburg, the whole time praying. These were not just ghost stories, these were real life horror stories. The spirit of Rosa Carmichael was still poisoning and torturing children over a hundred years later.

Summer was fuming as she continued ranting and raving, "Psychics, all they ever did was identify that Rosa was there and did nothing to get rid of her. How many lives have been ruined because of Rosa? How many are still being tortured and poisoned and don't even know why?"

Summer couldn't bear it. She had to get to Rosa! When she arrived at the Jennie Wade parking lot, Summer asked God where to go and she was led to The Gettysburg National Cemetery.

"General, come quick, it's *THAT* woman again!" the Lt. Colonel Jameson shouted to the General.

Knowing exactly what woman the Lt. Colonel was referring to the General sighed and asked, "What is she doing now?"

The Lt. Colonel, almost afraid to tell his superior officer the truth, spoke up and said, "She is at the National Cemetery again, Sir, and this time she is calling for Rosa?"

"What the....," the General came close to swearing.

He then gathered some of his Unknowns and off to the cemetery they went. Since time and space do not exist in the spirit world as humans know it to be, the General's spirit form was by Summer's side in a split second of time. Since, he was on hallowed ground, showing oneself to a human on such sacred ground was simply not a possibility. Summer did not know why she was at the cemetery, just that it was where God had sent her.

Pacing back and forth between the gravesites, an angry Summer shouted, "The spirit of Rosa Carmichael, in the name of Jesus, I command you to appear to me!"

The General and the Unknowns stood still as the spirit of Rosa Carmichael, and other disembodied spirits came out high above and in the middle of the two trees located behind the orphanage. It was like something out of a Frank Peretti book, "*This Present Darkness.*"[13] Rosa appeared just as Summer saw her in her vision — dressed as a witch and with her vial full of green poison.

The spirit said in a raspy voice, "You dare to tread on sacred ground, do you?"

The pungent smell of sulfur began to infiltrate the air around the demons hovering over Rosa, so much so that Summer started coughing as she demanded to know, "In the name of Jesus, what are your names?"

Due to the authority Summer carried in HIS name, the spirit of Rosa Carmichael *had* to answer. "Our names are Torture, Poison and Death!" Although Summer was almost choking due to the toxic air surrounding Rosa, the General was helpless and powerless to do anything about it.

Lumar, a wicked power of fear, said snickering, in a mockingly deep voice, "Oh look at her, a frail little human who thinks she can take us on."

While other imps joined in to ridicule Summer, Torture, Poison, and Death began to taunt the General, "Let us see you help her now, General Michael Moses McDaniels."

Just then, a Ministering Angel of Help named Horatius, with a wingspan of what looked like twenty feet in diameter, swooped down and said to Summer, "*For*

311

we are not contending against flesh and blood, but against the principalities, against the powers, against the rulers of this present darkness, against the spiritual hosts of wickedness in the heavenly places."

It was a scripture in the bible – Ephesians 6:12. A demon of anger hissed at the Angel Horatius as he covered Summer with his wings. The light beaming off the Angel blinded the demon of anger, causing it to recoil. While screeching, the demon of anger faded behind the trees in hopeless defeat. Just then, powerful and enormous warrior Angels, at least eight feet tall, appeared like shooting stars in the cemetery, by the thousands, with their mighty swords drawn! The Gatekeeper, upon hearing Summer Ray shouting, went to the window to look outside to see what the commotion was all about. With eyes as big as saucers, the Gatekeeper watched the great Heavenly beings descend on the lawn of The Gettysburg National Cemetery.

Philip, an Angel of Peace assured the General, "The *SPIRIT* has desired for Rosa to be eliminated for a very long time. This brave little warrior has been sent to do just that. Because she knows who she is in Christ,

312

and what His shed Blood represents, the demons must flee from her. Do not worry, though she suffers, Summer will overcome."

As the Angel Horatius helped her regain her bearings, Summer defiantly stood boldly before Rosa with both fists in the air and screamed, "How dare you hurt and torture those orphan children! How dare you continue to torture and poison innocent lives! In the name of Jesus Christ of Nazareth, you foul demonic spirit of Rosa J. Carmichael, I send you to the abyss to live, bound in chains, until God Himself sends you to Hell!"

Suddenly, the warrior Angels standing by took to flight and as their heavenly radiance filled the cemetery, Summer was knocked down by the force of their invisible strength as she could not see them but felt their power first hand. They grabbed the spirit of Rosa Carmichael, chained her and dragged her out of Gettysburg. Demons were screaming and shrieking at the sight of them. Disembodies and orbs were sent hurling from the presence of these great Heavenly beings. With lightning speed, Rosa was carried off, never to be seen or heard from again around Gettysburg.

Watching the scene in pure terror was the disheartened Woeburn. He knew he could be sent to the abyss as easily as Rosa. Clinging to "The Genius of Liberty," after the Angels dragged Rosa out of Gettysburg, he wheezed his putrid disgust and dug his talons into an inferior demon Lortob. Woeburn then threw Lortob into the statue like a rag doll. He needed someone to vent his rage upon and the Underworld does not have qualms about attacking its own.

"*He who is in you is greater.*" The Angel Horatius reminded Summer. Rory, Summer's guardian Angel, walked Summer out of the cemetery back to her car, with the General following close at hand as usual.

Back on the grounds of the Lutheran Theological Seminary, Captain Talhelm, told his heavenly host, "The *SPIRIT* has informed me the Underworld will once again launch an all-out war against Summer Ray."

Sostar screamed out, "Woeburn! We can take him out!"

Captain Talhelm reminded his over-zealous subordinate, "There must be more prayer support, or we will not be able to withstand him." The Captain then issued an order to the Angel Horatius, "Go to Kathryn Black and stir up a spirit of intercession in her and in the other prayer warriors at the Community Assembly of God in Frederick."

Horatius replied, "At once Captain!" Immediately, he flew off toward Frederick, Maryland.

Captain Talhelm then ordered Sostar, "Sostar, you will need to follow him in case he meets opposition. Horatius will be passing through small towns, where that spirit of slavery is still in operation and where much evil resides due to racism."

Sostar responded sarcastically, "Indeed Captain. The **KKK** in those areas must not have been informed of their African - American President." Then he too, took to flight and instantly met up with Horatius.

War Is Hell

A Confederate Unknown asked the General, "Does she know, Sir?"

General McDaniels responded, "I do not believe so!" Summer while concentrating on removing Rosa Carmichael, did not know nor perceive at the time, that she was actually standing amongst the gravesites of the fathers of the orphans who Rosa had tortured after the Civil War. Some of those fathers were the Unknowns that Summer met on Big Round Top. All Summer knew was that Rosa would never torture another one, and that was fine with her. But what she also didn't know was that the principality, Woeburn, as ordered by his master, the devil, was once again pursuing her.

A Union Unknown said to the General, "If she thinks you are bad, Sir, just wait until she has to come face to face with Woeburn!"

Although an Angel assured the General that Summer would overcome, the thought of Woeburn unsettled him. The General and his Unknowns were not supernatural beings like the dark creatures or the Light powerful beings. He did not know if he could help Summer, should this all-out war against her become a reality. The thought of it unnerved him because he knew he could not help her outside of the town of Gettysburg.

316

Summer lived only thirty minutes away in Maryland, but to the General, it might as well have been the moon. He knew he was strictly forbidden to leave Gettysburg. He could only hope this plot against her would happen within the limits that constrained him.

The General turned to his Unknowns and said, "In the words of General George Washington,

" War is hell."[14]

The General McDaniels, continued, "There is always an unseen battle going on between Light and dark. Though many people do not acknowledge it, it is for certain the God's honest truth. Those people who do not believe that He exists would surely believe it if they saw what we witnessed here tonight."

As Summer drove out of Gettysburg, Rory was sitting beside her. Summer was simply too drained to hang around the town. Her thoughts drifted back to Sam. Though she only met him once, it was enough for her to know she was crazy about him. There was something magical about their encounter. Summer couldn't put her

317

finger on it, but she knew it was heavenly. Still, she didn't have the slightest clue as to how to explain her life to him. Sometimes too crazy, really is too crazy and some realities are better left unsaid. Summer thought to herself,

"The General didn't show himself tonight." Summer not realizing she was accompanied by a rather glorious escort, began to pray,

"Father, in Jesus Name, I do not know what I am doing. But thank You for removing that wicked Rosa from that town and for helping those who were hurt by her to be restored. Thank You for Your Heavenly beings who came to help me. I don't remember what I know I need to. So, please help me to remember. It is haunting me and hurting me at the same time. The dreams are haunting me. Father, the General, I don't know what he is talking about — the promise I made. How could I have made such a promise? Even if I could remember, no one but You can bring peace and justice to those men. But You know my passion for Jennie and Jack. Please help! In Jesus Name...Amen"

318

Magnificent

What started out as a dull headache after she left the cemetery turned out to be the most excruciating headache she ever had, once she returned home. Pain exploded through the back of her skull as if someone had hit her with a sledge hammer. The left side of her face, neck and head felt like it was on fire. As Summer lay whimpering on the floor, trying desperately to stop even a morsel of pain, she didn't take in to account that all this agony was caused by a slithering python demon whose name was Constrict. Another demon named Phantor, a demon of backlash, with long tentacles, and an arched furry back, also followed Summer home, as ordered by their prince, Woeburn.

Spiritual Warfare of this magnitude, if not for the precious Blood of Jesus, would surely have cost this frail little human her life. As a frail little human in the eyes of Hades, is after all, a frail little human. The *SPIRIT* informed Talhelm that Rory, Summer Ray's Guardian Angel, was in need of assistance and Talhelm immediately dispatched warrior Angels to remove Constrict and Phantor.

319

With swords that glistened with the awesome power of God Himself, massive warrior Angels were confronted with the horrifying sight of seeing the python, Constrict, wrapped around Summer's head. With one swift blow, the Warrior Angel, Joel sliced the python spirit in half, causing it to thrash about in torment. Warrior Angel, Micah fought against Phantor and also prevailed. Phantor was cast out and sent back to his evil prince, Woeburn in Gettysburg. Even the demons believe there is a God and tremble. Yet until the end of time, they will not cease to harm as much humanity as demonically possible.

As Summer's migraine began to subside, she quietly thanked God for helping her. She then started praising Him for His goodness in getting rid of witchy Rosa Carmichael. The Angels sent to her aid began to praise the Lord with her.

"Hail to King Jesus. Praise be to the Lamb." Those words were sung by thousands of Angels in unison in the spirit world, this was something the dark powers hated more than anything else. They absolutely detested and despised the sound of praise to the Jesus who defeated them. They flee from any worship of the God who cast them out of Heaven, HIS Heaven! No wonder rebellion and pride are such an abomination to the Lamb. Those two traits are what caused the most beautiful of all Angels, Lucifer, to start a war in heaven.

Amazing, isn't it? Before war ever came to planet Earth, war was first authored by the devil, in Heaven of all places. Pride causes the most horrendous of results, as the devil and a third of the angels who followed him found out. Even a frail little human like Summer Ray, understands how incredibly stupid it is to try and out do God. He is just too magnificent! Lucifer forgot that he was a created being, and created beings can never beat nor become the Creator who created them.

Suddenly, Summer felt the comfort of the Holy Spirit within her and she was able to at least begin to fall asleep on the floor where she collapsed. She had been too weak to crawl into her bed upstairs after the demons attack.

"Sleep Little Warrior, sleep." Rory whispered to an exhausted and battle-scarred Summer Ray Sherwood.

Max, Summer's faithful German Shepherd, came and laid down beside her. Inspired by the Angel Horatius, Kathryn Black and other intercessors had already begun to pray for Summer Ray. Undoubtedly, Kat would soon be checking up on her friend. The Angels, standing guard around Summer and her home, noticed the feeble like state Summer was in, and it concerned even them.

Sostar spoke to Rory and said, "My dear friend and fellow comrade, I do not envy you having to watch your own go through something of this degree. When she suffers, you suffer."

The Angel Rory confidently answered, "Yes! But when she prevails, I rejoice."

Sostar replied, "Yes, *when* she prevails."

Rory told Sostar smiling, "The Lord is faithful Sostar. Her faith in Him is strong. She will prevail because of it."

The brave Warrior Angel answered, "Yes! We will have to fight to make sure of it!"

Rory reminded Sostar, "That is why we are here, to make sure of it!"

"The Lord, He is good Rory! He will make sure of it!" Sostar said looking down at a sleeping Summer.

"It seems as if Max will, too." Rory jokingly said to Sostar. Summer's phone rang. It was Kat on the other end.

Summer rolled to get to her cell phone and said, "Hello!"

A frantic Kat asked, "Summer, are you okay? I felt I really needed to pray for you this afternoon. You haven't answered the phone all day, so I also called the prayer chain at church."

Summer, leaving the casting out Rosa part on purpose answered, "I am fine. I just had a bad headache. It is better now. Thanks."

Kat asked her worn out friend, "Are we going to do the Jennie Wade tour tonight?"

"Of course!" Summer replied and continued, "That is if we can get the RIGHT tickets this time." She laughingly said to her friend.

Kat shot back to her, "You KNOW, it wasn't my fault!"

Summer responded back, "I know Kat. I know! I am just messing with you. Can you please drive tonight? I am really burnt out from this migraine."

Not knowing Summer was just in Gettysburg casting out a rather foul demonic Rosa Carmichael, Kat asked, "Are you sure you are up to going back to Gettysburg tonight?"

Summer immediately said, "I have to go."

Kat having heard those words before, knew it was pointless to try and talk her friend out of going. When Summer *had* to do something, she did it, even if the results were not necessarily to her benefit.

Kat then replied, "Okay Summer. I will pick you up at 7:00PM. That should give us enough time to get tickets and get something to eat before the tour at 9."

"Thanks! You really are the best!" Summer told her friend.

Before she hung up the phone, Kat replied, "Anytime Summer, and see you in a few hours."

Hearing Summer's conversation with her best friend, Sostar turned to Horatius and Rory then

324

informed them, "Well, it looks like we are going back to Gettysburg tonight."

Rory answered first, "Yes, and to the Jennie Wade house. I am sure there will be a battle."

Sostar and Horatius just smiled their Warrior smiles, as they loved to fight and defeat the demons.

Sostar told Rory, "We will meet you in Gettysburg my friend. We must return to the Captain to get our orders."

"Godspeed!" Rory said as Sostar and Horatius took to the sky toward Gettysburg.

Summer called for her dog, "Max, come on, boy. It's a beautiful day. You don't need to be inside."

Summer grabbed her Bible, sat down on the couch and began to read the Psalms. She wasn't sure what the Jennie Wade house would bring – a disgruntled General or an evil spirit trying to bring her harm. It was always best to be saturated in God's Word no matter what the reason. Still groggy from the migraine, Summer could barely concentrate on the Word. Her mind was racing a mile a minute over the events of that morning.

Summer asked herself, "Did I actually cast out Rosa? Wow! No wonder I had what felt like a sledge hammer to my head."

Summer then said out loud hoping all Underworld could hear, "The devil doesn't like to lose. Oh well devil, it sucks to be you! Doesn't the BIBLE also say something like, *If God if for us, who can be against us?* Oh wait, let me read some more... *The God of peace will soon crush Satan,* that's you, *under our feet.*"

Summer, just having to mock the devil more, went and grabbed a black sharpie and wrote the word "Satan," literally under her feet. She then stood up and began stomping her feet on the ground, crushing Satan under her, and rejoicing in its victory. After reminding him where he would spend eternity compared to where she would spend eternity, Summer finally felt content. Her God was with her and she knew it.

CHAPTER SIXTEEN

Devil's Den

"But your evilness, she is a Blood bought child of the Most High God. You know you cannot touch her. She is too heavily guarded. Just look at what those beasts did to Constrict and Phantor."

The demon said as he squealed before his prince trying to reason with him.

Dogwood chimed in, "Yea boss! They look as if they have just come out of a meat grinda."

The meeting with Woeburn and his "subordinate, inferior, lowlifes," as he liked to address them, was located at none other, Devil's Den. To this day it is called, "The Valley of Death." During the Civil War, thousands of men perished there. Plum Creek, at the base of the valley, flowed red with their blood. Devil's Den was a morbid point of interest for sightseers to gaze upon the bloody carnage, after the Gettysburg battle days. Confederate soldiers could be seen decomposing in the hot summer sun, sprawled out and slumped over rocks, in between the crevices of the rocks, or out in the fields in every position imaginable. They were left there to rot, as they were considered the enemy on Union soil. Some of their remains were washed away by the rain that followed the battle.

It has been said after every major battle, torrential rains come. Why this happens, one can only speculate. Perhaps it is God's way of washing the blood and gore away. The Battle of Gettysburg was no exception. The conflict, bringing so much mayhem on the tiny unsuspecting town, preceded three days of torrential downpours. There were three days of rain for three days of battle. Yet, the carnage seemed to have grown worse with the rains. As swollen bodies and detached limbs were washed away, creeks turned red from blood. Insects, birds and other animals ate of the flesh of the rotting corpses.

It's no wonder it is called "Devil's Den" as only something so dark as the devil himself could have masterminded such a malicious and insufferable war. What a castle is to a king, "Devil's Den" is to the princes of darkness. It is their fortified meeting place, as only dark powers are comfortable with death.

A Confederate ghost named William was watching the meeting from a nearby rock. He didn't dare make a sound. He knew his place. He was the ghost of a Confederate soldier, disgruntled that he was still on Union soil. But, even he did not mess with such dark beings as these. The General had often tried to help William find resolve, but William always refused. Time for him hadn't passed. He was still a Confederate soldier fighting for the South.

A House Divided

Slavery, though abolished, remained a sore subject, for both the Northern Union advocates as well as the Southern Confederate ones. The South, a proud and distinguished people, needed the slaves to work their rich farms and plush plantations. There are many theories, and actual documentation, as to how some of the

Southern slaves were treated. In the Revolutionary War, General George Washington's closest companion was a slave. During the Civil War, though hidden in most history books, even parts of the North had slaves. Despite the fact that slavery was not the actual reason for the Civil War, it played a role in desensitization of the South.

Caroline Turner, wife of retired judge Fielding Turner, were both friends of President Lincoln's wife's (Mary Todd's) family. Caroline, born in Boston, and the daughter of a well to do family, had the same sadistic mind as Rosa Carmichael. Where Rosa beat and tortured children, Caroline Turner beat and tortured slaves. Both of these women found something they cherished and became possessed with their own devilish brutality.

Slavery was a scourge that needed to be destroyed. Abraham Lincoln once stated on June 16, 1858:

> "*A house divided against itself cannot stand. I believe this government cannot endure permanently half-slave and half-free. I do not*

330

expect the Union to be dissolved. I do not expect this house to fall, but I do expect it will cease to be divided. It will become all of one thing or all of another."[15]

Yet, Lincoln also stated on August 22, 1862 in a letter he wrote to Horace Greeley:

"My paramount object in this struggle is to save the Union, and is not either to save or to destroy slavery. If I could save the Union without freeing any slave, I would do it, and if I could save it by freeing all the slaves I would do it; and if I could save it by freeing some and leaving others alone I would also do that. What I do about slavery and the colored race, I do because I believe it helps to save the Union, and what I forbear, I forbear because I do not believe it would help save the Union. I shall do no less whenever I shall believe what I am doing hurts the Cause, and I shall do more whenever I shall believe doing more will help the Cause."

President Barack Obama, on February 11, 2009 at Ford's Theatre where President Abraham Lincoln was assassinated, stated the following:

> *"For despite all that divided us, – North and South, black and white – he had an unyielding belief that we were, at heart, one nation and one people."*

And so, because of President Abraham Lincoln's unyielding belief, the South seceded from the Union and started their own Confederacy. On April 12, 1861, the Confederates fired on Fort Sumter. So, began the great American Civil War which left behind in its wake, a bitter divorce between North and South. It was a hatred so fierce that it devoured lives, homes and lands with death and destruction such had never been witnessed on American soil.

The First Essential

Years after that great and dreadful Civil War, the Gettysburg Confederate and Union Unknown Soldiers stood united, though invisible, under a *"flag of truce."*[16] They may have fought as enemies, but they were buried as brothers. Still, William didn't see a truce as a good thing. It was the reason the tainted creatures didn't bother him. They knew he was full of loathing hatred for anything good. The demons considered William to be one of their own, shoeless and all!

Woeburn growled, "We caused an accident years ago, did we not? Where was her God then?" he asked as he punched his fist through a rock.

A demon reminded him, "Yea, Boss, but she recovered and became stronger than ever in warfare, your great evilness."

Another imp squeaked in with the scripture, *"All things work together for good to those who love God."* You know, my lord, how Summer Ray loves the *ENEMY.*"

Woeburn turned around so fast, lashing at him with his tail, that the little imp didn't have time to react.

333

He was thrown so far into the night sky that he was just a blur.

Woeburn snarled, "It has been reported to me that she has an interest in Sam. He is her weakness. We will use him to get to her."

An Unknown scout, nearby at Devil's Kitchen, heard what Woeburn had said about causing Summer Ray's accident, and immediately reported it back to the General on Big Round Top.

"General, Sir! I overheard Woeburn reminding his demons that they caused Summer's car accident. She was telling the truth, Sir. Summer cannot remember her promise."

Though the General already knew the truth, it was still painfully sharp to hear. His actions against her were not that of a man of solid character. As he also knew General George Washington once stated:

> "*Good moral character is the first essential in a man.*"[17]

Though now a ghost, he was still a man nonetheless. Light and darkness, good and evil, past and future, destiny and fate, life and death – somehow were all meeting together at this particular place and time. The thought of it even scared the General as he knew the dark powers were going to try to stop Summer from remembering her past. He just did not know why. What he did know was that he had to somehow help her remember it. It was the only way he knew to bring peace.

If it was possible for a ghost to soul search, the General sure was doing enough of it himself. He thought of how he treated Summer, as if he were a demon himself. He was bitter, hateful and angry, especially at women. Summer was right and he knew it. The General had not forgiven his ex-wife for leaving him, nor had he forgiven himself for a weak moment that he believed had cost his men their lives. Bitterness made men full of poison, the kind of poison that Rosa spread around. He was beginning to see himself as he really was and it gnawed at him.

CHAPTER SEVENTEEN

The Gift

Summer noticed the word "séance" on the tickets for the Jennie Wade tour and instantly flashed back to a sermon at church. Her pastor was preaching on witchcraft, and how God's servants were not supposed to have anything to do with it. Summer, a "White Witch," or a psychic, while growing up, already knew she wasn't supposed to interact in séance's. She steered clear of the midnight tour. However, especially in Gettysburg, many a psychic claim they have "The Gift." In reality, all they have are mythical legends and folklore tales, deceiving the unsuspecting tourist. A select few ghost tour guides like to "twist history," adding historical information that never existed. They even try to make every sight and sound a make-believe ghost.

Some of the ghost tour guides even claim status as a high ranking "White Witch." That was something to think about as there was no such thing. A witch is still a witch, no matter what color you try to accent it with. It is one of the devil's greatest deceptions. Millions of people every year see *real* psychics to get a glimpse of their futures. When the psychic exposes a hidden truth, or reveals something about to happen, good or bad, and it does, it causes the unsuspecting person to be caught – hook, line and sinker. When confronted with the reality of the truth, behind the psychic, oftentimes the one revealing the truth is faced with great opposition. It is hard to accept something so genuine and so insightful could have its roots originated in the devil. But he is the mastermind of it. God said to have "*no fellowship with the unfruitful works of darkness, but rather expose them.*"[h]

Hell

These days, because of the state of the world, almost everyone wants to get in touch with the supernatural to find out what is going to happen to them. But it is never a good idea to find out from the dark side what is going to happen. Even if it is something good, if it came from the devil, it has the potential to lead a human soul straight to Hell. Hell was never meant for humans. It was only meant for the devil, his fallen angels and the disembodied spirits or demons.

Yet, how many countless number of human souls are in Hell, awaiting eternal damnation in a lake of fire? How many countless number of souls are already locked away behind bars − while demons stomp on them, rats eat at them, and souls cry out for cool, fresh air to breathe? It is a bottomless pit of endless foul odors, demonic torture, and wretched torment, and the darkness has full domination over the human souls that are carried there after their earthly expiration.

Their souls now belong to the darkness. It is a forever and without end punishment of all souls who did not accept Jesus Christ as their personal Lord and Savior. Lost souls burning in a lake of fire, while demons add more fuel to an already blazing inferno of brimstone every second of every day, with souls waiting for their final death to come and it never does, as a soul cannot die. It was not created by the Creator to die.

Those same demons that deceive, that oppress, depress and possess a human soul, take great pride and delight in dragging a human soul to Hell. It is the reward of their Master's approval that they love so much. Yet those same souls had every opportunity while alive on planet Earth to get it right. They heard the Word, knew of the Lamb, they just didn't want to receive Him. Even the atheists must have caught a glimpse of Him somewhere, but just couldn't see the truth of who He was. That is why it is so important for the servants of God to pray for eyes to be opened to the reality of the darkness.

Imagine, a loved one forever tormented in a lake fire, wishing for another death that will never come, just eternal damnation. Imagine a loved one having to smell the most hideous, gruesome, foul and repulsive smells forever. That isn't even the worst part of Hell. Souls will remember the many times God reached out to them to try and save them from such a horrible fate. They will remember their friends and family who tried to share the gospel with them and they refused it.

Such sadness can never be put into words. It is like forever reliving the Battle of Gettysburg and the aftermath, over and over and over again, for all eternity. No human being alive today can even imagine the atrocities of that war, let alone how they actually do relate to Hell. If General George Washington himself once stated that "*war is hell*," there must be some truth to it.

The Jennie Wade Tour

Summer and Kat arrived at the Jennie Wade house a little early, giving them ample time to finally eat at O'Rorke's, located directly across the street. Once inside the restaurant, due to the welcoming staff and the friendly restaurant patrons made Summer and Kat instantly feel at home. After their delicious nachos and iced tea, they still had a little time left to kill before the Jennie Wade tour. Kat and Summer decided to just walk around the town, soaking in the warm, summer air and ambiance of the famous town of Gettysburg.

While walking on Steinwehr Avenue, they passed by tourists of every shape, size and age. The ghost tour guides were all dressed up in Civil War attire, leading their groups throughout the town of Gettysburg with their lanterns fully lit, and telling ghost stories trying their best to intrigue or frighten those on their tours.

Summer and Katie stopped and said "hi" to Jeff, who owned a horse and carriage. Summer talked more to the horse than she did to Jeff. Her mind was wandering up the street to the store where she had met Sam, wondering what he was up to. But fear of the unknown kept her from asking. She knew he noticed her. Still, everything about him seemed too good to be true.

Summer was not up for more disappointment. So, she stayed close to the horse until Kat was almost done her conversation with Jeff, at which point, an impatient Summer Ray interrupted and said, "Come on, Kat! We have to get to the tour!"

Summer's lack of patience was never one of her finest qualities. But as soon as she said the words, "Come on" Summer saw a flashback to her college days. As her thoughts traveled back to a past time, when Kat saw the expression on Summer's face and she wondered if all the excitement was starting to shut Summer down again.

Kat said, "Summer Ray?" as she began to shake her. Meanwhile a demon named Sidetrack, hovered over Summer, trying to distract her from remembering her past. Almost instantly, an Angel of Serenity began to fill her mind with thoughts of peace. The pain subsided and Summer just kept on walking as if nothing happened. While Kat kept pondering all that was taking place, "Someone had to remember," she thought.

By the time they reached the Jennie Wade house, the tour was already gone!

Summer told her best friend, "So much for us being punctual. I have a feeling we will both be late for our own funerals."

Kat said laughing, "UH that would be a good thing."

They were directed to another tour which was already at the orphanage. The ghost tour guide was phenomenal. She acted out scenes of what she was portraying and made the stories even more fascinating. The tour crossed Baltimore Street and headed up to

Cemetery Hill. Due to the time of night, no one was permitted to cross into the park land, or they would be faced with hefty fines.

Summer, being the bold and adventurous woman that she was told her friend, "I think at least one fine would be worth it, just to hang out around the hill after midnight. But with the scary tales of that crazy woman trying to find her dead husband, I am not sure it would be *THAT* worth it!"

Kat and Summer both laughed. It was good to finally giggle and relax. With all that was going on, laughter gave them both a sense of assurance that God was with them. As the tour finally made it to the Jennie Wade house, an anxious General McDaniels was close at hand, wondering what Woeburn had in store. The spirit of Rosa Carmichael was one of his best rulers, poisoning and torturing thousands of lives. Woeburn was none too happy with this pitiful creature named Summer, and he was commanded to "*steal, to kill and to destroy*"[d] by his master, Satan. Angelic hosts were made aware of the plot against Summer by the *SPIRIT*, and they were ordered by Him to protect her and her friend, while at the Jennie Wade House.

Captain Talhem spoke to his Angelic Warriors, "Finally! Prepare for action, as tonight there is going to be a battle. My only concern is prayer support. The stronger they are praying, the stronger we are able to fight. It is an important lesson that many of the saints of God have yet to learn. The less they pray, the less we are able to accomplish."

Warrior Angels cried out, "PRAISE THE BLOOD OF THE LAMB."

The first part of the house visited was the cellar where a dead Jennie lay. It was somewhat chilling. Part of Jennie's fake hand actually looked as if it were a real dead hand, covered in dough, sticking out from underneath the patch quilt blanket that covered her. Cellars are cold, dark and damp! They are dusty, moldy and closed in. While the ghost tour guide told the story of Jennie Wade, the hair stood up on Summer's neck and all of a sudden she had a feeling of fear and dread wash over her, as those two slithering demons crawled in, unaware to her and to the rest of the group. Summer mistakenly thought it was the General trying to frighten her.

No one was near the rocking chair that sat beside a dead Jennie when it started to rock back and forth. The chain that hung in front of Jennie and the chair that separated them from the tour also started to sway back and forth. When the ghost tour guide turned the lights to the cellar off, all at once, chaos began to happen. Disembodied spirits, the General, some of his soldiers and warrior Angels all met inside the cellar, in the unseen spirit world. As camera lights began to pop, the tour group was startled by dark shadows and other electric energies that they perceived to be orbs and nothing more.

Filled with fear and dread, Summer began to panic. She was never one to like being closed in, as she hated the feeling of not being able to get out. She didn't stop to think demons were oppressing her which she could have, rebuked in the name of Jesus. Demons have a way of concealing themselves so that humans think their oppression is caused by something else. It is almost like a twofold curse. Humans tend to fight the wrong things and never get the freedom they so desperately need. If a demon is what is causing the ailment, it is the demon that needs to be cast out. But, far too often, deliverance is overlooked, especially in some Christian circles. It is sad, so terribly sad.

Still not realizing her fear and dread were caused by demons, Summer just wanted to get to the cellar door as quickly as possible. Summer's heart began to race again and fear of another attack like Rosa Carmichael engulfed Summer in terror. As she began to quiver, weep and hyperventilate, the demons attacking her were filled with excitement at seeing her so fragile and pathetic. Blocked by others in the tour who were still snapping pictures in the dark, Summer was shutting down. She was hoping to hold onto Kat to find some comfort until she could get outside. But her friend was also caught up in the crowd and Summer didn't know where she was.

In times of crisis, humans have a tendency to forget what they cannot see, as emotions begin to take over, where rational thinking should be in control. The devil knows that human emotions are strong. Emotions can also work against a human and become a weakness, if they are used in the wrong way. Summer was too naïve to think the devil had such knowledge of the human heart. Emotions of fear and panic were demonic strongholds in Summer's life and were operating in full force trying to get her to breakdown.

As warrior Angels were engaged in battle with these and other demons, the General grabbed Summer's right hand as if to let her know that he was there. When she felt pain but didn't see anyone touching her, she instinctively knew who it was. This in fact, caused her to be even more afraid. If it wasn't the General who caused all this fear and dread, who was it?

When the cellar doors were finally opened, Summer couldn't get outside fast enough. Breathing fresh clean air, Summer felt like a butterfly just let out of its cocoon. She met Katie on the steps in front of the house and wasn't sure if she was going to finish the rest of the tour. Something was terribly wrong and Summer, like a deer caught in the headlights, knew that something was upon her. This was the one tour she desperately wanted to go on, so she decided to get a grip and just go through with it, all the while silently praying to God to protect them from whatever it was that was harassing her.

The General could see Summer hadn't left the tour, so he stayed close by.

This wasn't Jennie's real house. It actually was one that Georgia, her sister, was renting. But, with so much firing going on in the distance where Jennie had lived on Breckenridge Street, Jennie decided it was best to take her brother, Harry, and their young boarder, Isaac, to stay at Georgia's house for better protection. Samuel, Jennie's brother, chose to stay at a neighbor's house, nearby.

Jennie Wade, the true American patriot, had been bringing water and baking dough to the Union soldiers near Cemetery Hill. But, on the morning of July 3, 1863, the third day of the Gettysburg battle, as she was kneading dough, a Confederate sharpshooter shot a minie ball through both the front and parlor doors, hitting Jennie in the back, right beneath her left shoulder blade. The bullet pierced her heart, killing her instantly. Jennie was on the left side of the kitchen when she decided to move to the right side, where she could close the parlor door to better protect herself. Had she remained on the left side, there is no evidence that she

349

would have been hit by a bullet, and so her life may have been spared. One decision cost her - her life. Yet, her patriotism will live on forever.

The floor boards, where Jennie's blood fell, were sold off and made into a windowsill. No one on the tour could quite understand why anyone would make a windowsill out of floor boards stained with Jennie Wade's blood, especially Summer! It didn't seem to bring her much honor.

"Maybe a museum would have been more appropriate," she thought.

There is a paper taped to the parlor door, with a picture of a newly married couple on their wedding day. Legend has it that if a single woman put her ring finger through the bullet hole in the parlor door, not the front door, as many mistakenly think, within one year she would be engaged or married! Summer's dream of marriage to the man that she was created for − the man whose rib was inside her chest − the man who took that sinking feeling away, and the man who made her soul jump for joy every time he looked at her, had yet to come true. But, she never gave up the hope that it would.

When a demon of sabotage noticed Summer put her left ring finger through the bullet hole, he immediately threw a candle across the room that hit the back wall, as if trying to stop fate and destiny from ever happening in Summer Ray's life.

When the ghost tour guide saw the flying candle, she asked Summer, "Do you have an angry ghost after you?"

It was then that Summer decided it was best to leave the tour. She didn't want others in the tour to possibly get hurt at her expense. Although Summer wasn't physically hurt, she was deeply hurt in her soul! Whoever it was that was causing the commotion was breaking her heart all over again, as the memories of her marriage came flooding back. Betrayal is a terribly hard thing to get over. Her ex-husband didn't have to be so brutal. But he was and there was nothing Summer could do about it. He was hell bent on ending the marriage so he could live with this other woman, who eventually left him for another man. When Tommy tried to reconcile, Summer simply laughed in his face. There is such a thing as going too far. Tommy, she thought, went too far.

But it still did not stop the memories. Oh, how she wished she could turn those off and turn on the memories of the promise she had made to the Unknowns. What would have possessed her, a twenty-one-year-old college student, to think she could bring peace to such a massive and devastating war? What did she see ten years ago on that hill? Where did Sam fit into all of this?

Little did Summer know, all the tumult was caused by the Underworld trying to tear apart her soul, and cause her to renounce her faith in the God she loves. The memories of the heartache and betrayal by her ex-husband were only expounded upon even more when Summer saw Sam crossing Baltimore Street near the tavern, with another woman close at hand. They were laughing, carrying on and looking as if they had known each other a long time. When Sam looked up and saw Summer Ray across at the Jennie Wade House, he must have seen the expression on her face as she abruptly turned around and ran up the parking lot to Kat's car. Upon seeing what sent Summer running, Kat put her head down and said, "Oh God, please, not again!"

352

CHAPTER EIGHTEEN

The Battle for Summer's Faith

A distraught Summer couldn't pray. She could only run as fast as she could away from Sam. When the General saw her and Kat drive out of town on Emmitsburg Road near the battlefields, he knew he was strictly forbidden to follow her home. He saw the despair in her eyes and the General, knowing he, too was the cause of it, could only sit there on his horse and watch Summer leave.

His cold and bitter heart was turning warm and tender toward this "scrawny woman," as he called her. As remorse and penitence filled his own heart, Summer Ray's was breaking all over again. Another betrayal she just couldn't bear, especially not with Sam. Summer's despair grew to the point she began to yell at God. When Kat heard her, she tried the best she could to console her friend, but to no avail. Summer was beyond consoling.

The drive home was one of delight for the dark powers. Yet, it came with great sorrow for the Light. This was the battle they had talked about, the battle for Summer's faith. They knew the darkness would do everything they could to destroy it and only Summer herself could make the choice to save it. It just didn't seem fair that the darkness could kill, steal and destroy it while the Light could only sit by at times and watch them do it. Summer didn't want to fall in love with Sam. She didn't even go looking for love. It just happened out of nowhere.

Once at home, she begged her friend to leave her alone. Kat promised, however, she would check in on her later. She had not seen Summer so lost since her divorce. What was it about betrayal and divorce that can kill a human life and destroy a human heart? This was worse than betrayal and divorce. The sinking feeling in Summer's stomach, though gone was, now replaced by a rather large hole. She knew God had sent her back to Gettysburg, but the betrayal she felt by her God was simply more than she could bear. Summer began weeping and wailing to the point she could no longer lift her head to Heaven. The God she loved more than life itself, the God she had never turned away from, somehow faded to black and white.

Summer ran to her study with nothing but books everywhere and she began to throw them off the shelves. She took her bibles and threw them in a box. The book she was typing she deleted off of her computer and then took down every picture in her house with a bible verse on it, and threw them in boxes, too. Meanwhile, the demons and principalities were throwing a party in her honor. They were rejoicing at the sound of her tears. They knew they had overcome her, finally, and they laughed, they danced and they worshipped their dark master, who was overjoyed with them. The demons knew she could not bear another heartache, even if the God she served did not. The powers of darkness knew they could break Summer's spirit. It was just a matter of time, as a frail little human is after all, a frail little human. Sam meant the world to Summer. Love, when it is real, can happen in a split second of time, just like it did with Summer's love for Sam.

As Summer cried out to the God she had thought deserted her, all she could say was, "How could You?

Did you send me back to Gettysburg just to get hurt AGAIN? What kind of a God are You? You let me almost die in a car accident. You let my husband leave me after he cheated on me. Finally, when I was starting to feel normal again, and happy to be alive, You send me to the most wonderful man I have ever met, only to have him reject me, too."

When Summer went to the medicine cabinet to get some narcotic pain medication, Nathanial, the Angel of Destiny, asked Rory, her guardian Angel, if he had done something wrong. It was he who directed Summer into the store where she met Sam.

Rory compassionately responded, "Since birth, the devil has tried to take this child's life one way or another. You know, it started when her mother, aunt and grandmother stood over her crib and dedicated that sweet innocent baby to the devil. Her road with the Lamb has been much harder than most because of it. The devil still has not let go of what he claims is his right to her. Though now a Blood bought child of God, the warfare for her soul is a greater price to the darkness that wins it. That is why there is so much turmoil surrounding her, and why the devil tries so hard to cause her despair. It was the SPIRIT'S will that led her to Sam. Though He has not shown us why, we can only hope that Summer will overcome, and remember that God is good."

When a demon of addiction saw Summer Ray take two pills instead of just one, he flew back to Hell to convince his ruler to allow him to bring more demons back with him. It was, "To make certain she would crumble under the pain and pressure, causing her to go even further down into the pit."

Addiction's ruling principality gladly obliged, and sent a demon of despair and one of crippling addiction, back to Summer Ray's house. After Summer took her narcotic pain medications, she told God that she would never go back to Gettysburg, and that she would never trust Him again.

When Kat called Summer to check up on her as promised, Summer cried to her, "How could God be so cruel as to purposely break my heart all over again?"

Immediately, a determined Kathryn called the prayer warriors at their church and called for an emergency meeting at her house. This was something the Angels were happy about.

Captain Talhelm told his heavenly host, "Now we can get to work. Even if Summer cannot lift herself up, the prayers of these other saints will allow us to battle on her behalf, until she is able to help herself. This is something the darkness did not count on, and not a moment too soon as Summer is already having thoughts of taking enough pills to end her life." The *SPIRIT* revealed this crucial information to another Angel.

When humans are in despair, they are like prey to the devil. They can sink so low into desperation that they lose all sense of hope. They are nothing more than meat to a demon trying to drag their soul to Hell. Even blood bought children of God can, and have, ended their own lives. If only they could just hold on. Yet, something so good and so wonderful can also crush a human heart to absolute death. The opening of one's heart to love, only to have it crushed again, makes it no wonder that humans fall deep into hopelessness.

Real love is a glorious thing to behold. But the devil hates the human heart. It has the ability to love, to give, to surrender, to be happy and to sing. He would rather destroy it and remove the human being from planet Earth. When the phone rang, Summer hesitated to answer it. But when she saw it was Tommy's phone number, she knew she had to.

A groggy Summer said, "Hello?"

"Hi, Mom, it's Billy. I miss you, Mom. I will be home in a few days."

Billy didn't let his mom get a word in edgewise. He was so excited about his camping trip. With the sound of his voice, and the words from her son, Summer started to cry all over again.

Billy asked worriedly, "Mom, what's wrong?"

Summer told her anxious son, "Oh nothing, I just miss you too. I am glad you are having a good time."

A concerned Billy said, "Ahh, Mom, don't cry."

Just then, Tom took the phone and said to her, "Here he was, having a great time, and you had to go and ruin it. He will be home Saturday morning," and with that, he hung up.

Summer didn't know it was an Angel inspiring Billy to call his mom. The SPIRIT knew her son would snap her out of wanting to commit suicide. As Summer hung up the phone, she put the extra pills back in the bottle. In fact, she decided to throw out all her narcotic pain medication. When a warrior Angel saw her flush her pills down the toilet, he slammed the demon of addiction into the ground. As the prayer group offered up more prayers, more of the Light was released, and came to assist the other warrior Angels. Though Summer could not bring herself to pray, she was at least safe from harming herself and no other demon was allowed to enter her house the rest of the night.

CHAPTER NINETEEN

The Past

There is nothing more agonizing than almost remembering and not being able to. So many pieces were trying to fall into place, it was a new kind of pain all over again. History, when you cannot remember it is almost cruel. Although, there are times when it is best to forget it. It is when it is most desperately needed to be remembered, that it becomes a living nightmare. Summer wanted to remember the snow, but just couldn't!

After Summer passed out from the medication and total exhaustion, her dreams took her to another new place, a place she never dreamed of before. She was only five years old, and Summer was learning how to ice skate. She was on a frozen pond in the middle of winter, somewhere in Gettysburg. Her dad was there, trying to teach her how to ice skate. He was so proud of his Summer Ray. She was born in June and her dad called her, "*The sunshine of my life.*" So, what better name could she have been gifted with?

There she was, on a pond with her little skating dress and the dumbest skates she had ever seen. Her dad knew the owners of the farm where they were skating. Every winter, for several years, they graciously allowed Summer Ray to ice skate on their pond. By the time she was ten years old, the winters stopped being cold enough to freeze the pond, and she had to stay at the ice rink.

After her accident at the age of twenty-three, she was told by her doctors that she might not ever skate again. She lost most of the feeling in her arms, hands, legs and feet. They told her she might end up permanently paralyzed, and that simply was too much for Summer Ray to bear. She told them all to basically go, "you know where," as the thought of not ever being able to ice skate again was worse than the thought of death itself. Tommy did the best he could with her injuries, but like General McDaniels, Summer was locked into her own private hell, and no one could break her free from it. When Tom told his wife not to skate, he was met with the same response she gave her doctors. It was Summer's life, and only she could determine its outcome.

In her dream, she saw herself skating for the first time since her accident. She had on skates that felt like dead weights, as she could not feel them on her feet. A once competitive skater, now here she was just learning how to march. One can never know, except for Summer, the amount of excruciating pain it had caused her, those millions of hours of practice, gone. It was as if she just a beginner, who could barely stand up in the same skates that once took her to flight. With her husband, coach, parents, and best friend at rink side, Summer took a step on the ice. It was almost a miracle, in motion as she fell repeatedly, only to get back up again. Before she left the rink that day, she was determined she was going to, at the very least, do a crossover.

It was like the time when she was learning how to ride a bike. She refused to go inside, even after ten hours of trying to learn. Somewhere around the fourteenth hour, she finally peddled that bike, and she finally was able to stay on it without falling off. Her parent's expression as they watched their baby girl refuse to give up and finally ride on her own, were beautiful to behold. It was especially hard on her dad, a she was daddy's little girl, and he kept trying to persuade Summer's mom to bring her inside.

He saw the bruises on his daughter's body every time she fell. Her knees were bloodied, and her face didn't look that great either, as it too, was scraped and bruised by the cement it landed on. But Summer wasn't a quitter, something her parents were grateful for. Once Summer rode her bike all the way down the street without falling off, she immediately went inside and asked for something to eat, as if nothing happened. Her mom and dad smothered her with hugs and kisses and told her how proud of her they were. She just wanted a piece of pizza.

Summer's older brother, Greg, also gave her a hug of approval, as he grabbed her around the neck and dug his knuckles into her head and said, "Good job, Squirt!"

Though Summer never fully regained all of the sensation in her body, and though for a time she had to stop competing, she still managed to work her way into becoming a Figure Skating Coach.

Once she put Billy on the ice, she learned about the sport of ice hockey. Summer then began to help some of the hockey players become stronger on their skates so they could play the game with more confidence. No! Summer Ray was not a quitter. But she was badly bruised inside her heart. The bruises on the outside were always so much easier to heal than the ones on the inside. This night Summer did not dream of big blue eyes and snow. She did not dream of wounded and dying soldiers, as it was her who was now wounded. She did not dream of Jennie or Jack and the possibility that history could be re-written to give them a happier ending. She did not dream of the General, who she thought was against her.

No! This night, Summer only dreamed of her past, a past she had not been able to remember in a very long time. Was it God trying to remind her of her determination to never quit? One can only guess. When Summer woke up the next morning, God had written on the tablets of her heart the following poem:

STILL

I am strong enough to say, "Goodbye."
But still weak enough to stay.
Never knowing how or why,
I loved you anyway.

Torn between the reality of,
The way things are right now.
Though many waters cannot quench love,
I, just do not see how.

Still, I see the truth behind your eyes,
And a promise of what could be.
Underneath the if's and why's,
There's just you and me.

Though impossible and greatly shattered,
Like a ship lost out at sea.
Tossed and torn and greatly battered,
There's still you and me.

Though I don't know how, and don't know when,
God for us will turn the tide.
Somehow, we'll be together again,
And forever be side- by - side.

Summer wasn't exactly sure who God had her write that poem for, General McDaniels, Sam or some other lost love she had yet to find. Love in Summer's life had remained to be seen. Yet, in the midst of so much confusion and heartache, it was best to wait until she was whole herself. Way too many people make decisions out of desperation. Desperate relationships rarely ever work out. The last thing Summer needed was another train wreck. Waiting was not just the best thing to do; it was the only thing to do.

The Truth

Kat didn't call Summer Ray. Instead, she just dropped by her house. When the doorbell rang, looking in the mirror at herself in shambles, Summer decided not to answer it. She temporarily let it slip her mind that her best friend had a key and decided to use it.

"Summer Ray, where are you?" Kat demanded.

When she found Summer in her study, she ran to her friend and hugged her. Summer was as distraught as she has ever seen her. Kat Black was not one to sit back and idly watch the world crumble around her best friend. She took Summer Ray to the kitchen and sat her down at the kitchen table.

Kat then made a pot of coffee and began to make Summer Ray breakfast as she continued speaking, "Now, tell me everything, Summer Ray Sherwood. Even the parts you left out that you thought I wouldn't understand or be too afraid to hear. The Lord revealed to us in prayer last night that you were keeping things from me, and that you were not able to handle things on your own."

It gave Summer a great sense of relief that she could finally unload to someone, and not just someone, but her best friend.

"Okay! I will tell you. But only if you promise to keep quiet until I am finished."

Summer even made her friend pinky swear. She knew Kat wasn't one to keep quiet about anything longer than two minutes. Summer began to unload what was in her heart, "You know part of the reason we went back to Gettysburg was because I went looking for the Colonel. You know he appeared to me in a dream and how he told me to, 'remember your promise.' When I woke up, I tried to find a General McDaniels on the Internet. I only found a Colonel McDaniels. I did not know what promise he was talking about, so I figured I'd go looking for him in Gettysburg. Do you remember when we were on the Orphanage tour and I was almost trapped in that cubby hole? I was attacked by the spirit of Rosa Carmichael, and later I sent her to the abyss."

Kat asked, "You sent her where? When?"

Kat was trying hard to not say a word and just couldn't help herself.

"Okay! So, tell me about the General. Is he cute?" an over curious Kat asked, still trying to be quiet.

Summer explained, "The General is quite possibly the most handsome man, or ghost, I have ever seen. He has black and graying hair, rugged and very defined. But he is a ghost who hates women because his wife left him during the Battle of Gettysburg. She went so far as to divorce him and remarry before the General had a chance to convince her otherwise."

Kat mumbled, as she poured their coffee, "Oh no, that is harsh...go on...go on."

Summer continued, "Well, do you also remember when I told you I was going out for a morning walk when we stayed at the Travelodge? That part wasn't exactly true. I drove to Big Round Top instead. I knew I would find him there and sure enough, I did. But what I didn't expect to see were thousands of US Unknown soldiers of the Civil War. I saw them! Some had the word "Unknown" written across their foreheads. The rest had numbers written across their foreheads. I could never understand the numbers. Even while walking through The Gettysburg National Cemetery, you know how much it grieved me to see Unknown soldiers marked only as a number."

Summer, looking out the kitchen window, was drifting off into a blank stare.

Kat shouted, "Summer! Focus!"

"Okay, okay!' Summer said and continued, "When I asked the General why he was haunting me, he told me I promised him I would be back. Not only that, but somehow, I also promised that I would do whatever I could to bring him and the Unknowns peace. He knew about the scars on my hand. I told him I didn't know how I got them. Then he called me a liar and I called him a 'bitter, angry, spirit who hated women'."

A surprised Kat asked, "You said what?"

Summer scolded her friend, "Hush will you! "I also called him a 'coward' and that's when he pinned me against a rock and kissed me so hard, I cried."

Kat interrupted and said, "Wait! What? He kissed you? How dare you keep that from me! Hold on! Now just wait a freakin' New York minute!"

Summer looked with her with arched eyebrows reminding Kat, "You hate New York!"

Kat shot back, "Shut up! He is a ghost, right? How can ghosts kiss? Aren't they transparent and without substance?" A confused Kat then asked, "How did a ghost find your mouth?"

Summer kept trying to explain, "The General, for whatever reason, can be seen in human form all over Gettysburg except the National Cemetery. The Union Lt. Colonel Jameson, and the Union and Confederate Unknown soldiers, can only be seen in human form on Big Round Top. It is a mystery the General did not explain. But right after he almost kissed my mouth off, he told me that if he hated so women so much, he would have let Rosa Carmichael suffocate me when she had her hands wrapped around my throat."

Kat looked at Summer as if she was either going to throw up or run. But curiosity kept her glued to her chair, as she was much too interested in the General and bombarded Summer with questions.

"So, he kissed you? What was it like? Was it a movie kind of kiss? You know — the kind of kiss where the guy takes the woman he loves in his arms, and kisses her passionately because he just can't live without her?"

Summer burst her best friend's romantic bubble when she replied, "No Kat! It wasn't a movie kind of kiss. It was an, 'I hate you! Get the hell off of my hill and don't ever come back' kind of kiss."

"Well that sucks! What the hell is wrong with him?" Kat demanded to know.

"You do realize we are talking about a freakin' ghost, here right? I am sure there is plenty wrong with him. I just don't know what. Do you see why I left out certain pieces? But he also said I was at Big Round Top ten years ago. I know you said I was there doing a college thesis. He said I cut my hand on a thorn bush. He knew about my scars. I don't remember cutting my hand on a thorn bush."

A curious Summer asked her friend, "Do you know anything about this?"

There was plenty her best friend knew about. Kat was silently hoping she wasn't going to have to explain about the trip to the Gettysburg hospital. Kat overheard Summer's parents tell the doctor treating their daughter's injured hand that she was adopted. Kat was turning green. She had to tell Summer the truth about the thorn bush.

Inwardly agonizing, hoping that is all she had to tell, Kat finally explained, "Yes, Summer. You did cut your hand open on a thorn bush. In fact, by the time I was able to crawl up the hill to get to you, you were going

373

into shock. You were seriously bleeding, and somehow you managed to cover your hand in snow."

Summer interrupted her, "It wasn't me who covered my hand. It was the General. He told me he did. He told me about you coming up the hill to rescue me. But what about the promise I made to him? Do you know anything about that?"

Kat confessed, "The truth is, I heard you mutter something about coming back and promising to bring peace. When I looked back to see who you were talking to, I didn't see anyone. I thought you were just delirious and paid no attention to it."

With that, both women began to cry as Kat told her friend, "I am so sorry I kept this all from you. I didn't know it meant anything."

Summer stood up and hugged her friend then asked her if there was anything else that she remembered about that day.

Feeling two feet tall, Kat lied, "Well, there is one more thing. On the way to the hospital, when we passed Devil's Den, there was a man on the side of the road. When he passed the SUV you put your hand up and touched the window as if you wanted to say something to him. But you were fading in and out of consciousness so I decided not to stop."

"Blue eyes, he had blue eyes!" Summer jumped back to her feet as if the prison door had finally just sprung open.

Kat asked, "Could it be Sam?"

A dejected Summer replied, "No! His eyes are a grayish color. I wish it was though. Now that would make for one hell of a fairytale!"

Kat replied, "Hello...Summer Ray! This whole story is turning out to be one hell of a fairytale."

Summer fell back down in her chair and put her face in her hands. The God who seemed so cruel yesterday seemed even more barbaric this morning.

"Why is God doing this to me?" Summer asked Kat as her tears began to fall again.

Summer then confessed to her friend, "Last night I had to throw away my pain medication. I thought of overdosing."

A terrified Kathryn Black screamed, "Summer no! Why didn't you call me?"

Summer replied, "Because it wasn't your battle Kat. You have to stop rescuing me. You said you all prayed, so maybe your prayers kept me from taking more pills. Thanks."

Kat asked her friend, "So, where do we go from here?"

Summer sadly spoke, "I don't know Kat. The General thinks I can somehow bring him and the Unknowns peace. Sam is with another woman. I have no reason to go back to Gettysburg."

Kat inquired, "What about Jennie and Jack?"

Summer responded with, "What about them? Like, I can really re-write history to give dead people a happier ending. It was a stupid idea to begin with. I haven't been able to find that for myself and I am alive. What makes me think I can do that for Jennie Wade?"

Kat then asked, "What about Sam? Have you heard from him?"

An unhappy Summer told her friend, "No! I don't really expect to either. I can't go back. I just can't. The General will never find me here. He and the Unknowns are not allowed to leave Gettysburg. Sam doesn't even know where I live. Jennie and Jack, well I don't have too much to worry about there!"

Kat could no longer stand Summer Ray's pity party when she glared at her and said, "This is not the Summer Ray I know. The Summer Ray I know defied the laws of nature, her doctors, her family and her friends. The Summer Ray I know isn't a quitter. What happened to her?"

Summer defended herself, "I don't know. I cannot bear the thought of Sam with another woman. It is like a bullet piercing my heart. I simply cannot bear it. It is too painful. God sent me right to him, but why? Was it to watch me get hurt and rejected again? Is that seriously the heart of God? Have I been so carelessly blind in believing in shallow crap that I missed the real God?"

Kat firmly told her friend, "Summer, you of all people know that God is good. It might be hard for you to say it now, but nonetheless, you know it is the truth. I do not understand why any of this is happening either. I have no idea. If I knew I would tell you, but God did not reveal His secrets to any of us who prayed last night, other than you were keeping things from me."

Kat then asked her distraught friend, "Do you honestly believe that God purposely sent you to Sam to hurt you?"

Summer replied, "Well, at first I thought God was finally allowing me to live my dream of getting married to the man I was created to love, the one who made me feel as if he were part of my own skin. Then, to be rejected by him, it was pain I could not bear. Did God know that would happen before He sent me to him? Of course! So, based on that information, God purposely sent me to Sam, knowing I would get hurt. Why? Was God using Sam to test my faith again?

Is that what all this was about, to see if I would bow my knee to Satan? When will it ever be enough for God? When will the faith I have already given to Him be enough? When will my allegiance to Him finally be satisfactory? God knows I would never bow my knee to Satan. I would never go back to witchcraft. So, when is it ever going to be enough? Do I have to continually prove my love for Him? It's getting old Kat, and I am simply tired of it. If God can't trust my love for Him by now, He never will. I know I won't ever go back to darkness. But after all of this, I am not sure I can go on with the Light. I seriously wonder what the point is. I do not ask God for much. I never have. But even you know, how I have dreamed of marriage. All my life, even as a little girl, it was all I ever dreamed about. Well, that and figure skating."

Summer finally laughed, then turned to Kat and asked, "Don't you remember how I used to play dress-up in my mom's wedding gown?"

Kat froze in her chair. Without realizing it, Summer was beginning to remember her childhood.

"Remember how we would sneak into her wooden chest when we were like ten years old? She was at work and I would put her dress and veil on. Remember at our tea parties we had our make-believe princes?"

The flood of Summer's memories had finally broken through when she continued speaking, "Do you remember those parties we would have up in the woods at our junior high school? Remember the time the cops came and we all went running and I ended up flipping over a barbed wire fence? Remember our first cigarette and how sick we both got and how much trouble we got in? I didn't know my mom actually counted her cigarettes."

Summer said laughing, "Oh and what about the time we were at the beach and a wave hit you so hard you lost your bikini top. I had to protect you from those boys who wanted to see. I believe I punched one of them. Oh, I miss those days Kat. You know, when life seemed so innocent."

Summer continued to reminisce, "But do you remember how I drove passed J&B Bridals in Chambersburg? For years I drove passed that store, and for years I knew the gown in the window was the one for me. I knew that even before Tommy left me. I just didn't understand the Civil War part of it, even though during the Civil War era women didn't actually have wedding gowns. You know how that gown looked like it belonged in the Civil War era. Remember when I tried it on and how picture perfect it was?"

Kat was watching a miracle and Summer Ray was actively unaware of it. When Summer looked at her friend, she had a weird, yet wonderful look on her face.

"What?" Summer asked, oblivious to what had just happened.

"You okay, Kat?" Summer was never one for patience.

Becoming frustrated Summer demanded to know, "What is wrong with you?"

Finally able to get a word in edge wise, Kat asked, "Summer, do you know what just happened?"

Summer, still clueless, acting as if nothing strange or unusual occurred said, "No not really, what?"

Kat told her best friend through her tears, "You remembered!"

Summer gave her a puzzling look and asked, "Remembered what?"

Kat, bursting with joy, exclaimed, "Your mother's wedding gown, smoking cigarettes up at Wood Jr. High School, our tea parties, you protecting me at the beach and J&B Bridal's in Chambersburg."

A now stunned Summer said, "Oh my God! I did," as she too began to cry. What she thought was forever buried and tragically lost, suddenly had been miraculously bestowed upon her. Rory, standing close by, was greatly relieved that Summer's memory had started to return. He knew the missing pieces of her past had to be revealed in order for her to accomplish her mission. He lifted a "thanks be to God" into the air and spoke softly in Summer's ear to go ice skating.

Your Place In History

Kat laughed, "I saw your office. We need to put it back together."

"Tomorrow!" an exhausted Summer said.

Kat asked Summer again, "Okay! But what about Gettysburg?"

Summer wearily replied, "I just told you why I cannot go back. I cannot keep a promise that I have no way of keeping. I cannot bring peace to dead soldiers. I cannot give Jennie and Jack a happier ending and I cannot bear the thought of Sam with someone else. I am just not that strong. Gettysburg will have to do without me. I will have to put my mind to the ice more, that's all. The ice always helps me recover."

Kat inquired, "Are you skating today?"

Summer nodded, "Yes, I think I should. The sooner I skate the sooner this will all go away. I am sorry if I have disappointed you. I know you were anxious to meet the General."

Kat said as she hugged her friend goodbye, "I am just glad you are safe Summer, that is all that really matters. So, go skate and call me when you get home!"

A demon gloated to a spirit of wickedness, "She still hasn't praised the Lord."

The spirit of wickedness bellyached his response, "Yes! But she hasn't renounced her faith either, and that will cause us trouble in the Underworld."

A demon of lament hissed, "If only those saints hadn't prayed, she would be ours by now!"

Summer Ray was seriously trying to keep her mind on her skating, but with the sappy love songs they were playing, it was kind of impossible. Sam was gone! There wasn't any way to just get over him and she knew it. The tears were going to fall regardless of how she tried to shut them off. The memories were going to hurt, no matter how much she tried not to remember. That was what was so sadistic about all of this. The things she needed to remember she couldn't and the things she needed to forget she couldn't. With time, Summer knew the pain would eventually subside, she just had to somehow keep herself busy, and out of Gettysburg.

Gettysburg was her pot of gold. It was where she found Sam. Although Gettysburg was an island unto itself, it was still only thirty miles from her home. It was still too close for comfort. Anytime she drove her car somewhere, there were always great big signs that read, "Gettysburg" with arrows pointing the way. What was she supposed to do, close her eyes while driving? If being haunted by the General wasn't bad enough, the fact that Sam was flesh and blood, still made her heart skip a beat. There simply were no words to describe the depth of love Summer Ray felt for him.

It is agonizing to wait for the sound of the phone to ring that never does. Anyone who has experience it knows full well it is a horrible way to live. The non-stop sorrow that is caused by feelings of being unwanted is just wasted sorrow on wasted time. Seriously, who has the time sit around and wait for the phone to ring when they can be creating a new life instead? Especially now, in the modern age of cell phones, there is simply no excuse to sit around moping and being sad all the time.

The sun still rises every morning like it always has, does it not? And who's to say, with the motivation to get going and to get busy with a new life, the cell phone you carry around won't be ringing with a call from the person you so desperately long to hear from? If you keep faith alive, that phone can, and eventually will ring. What an even greater surprise to how wonderful you are doing. But what an even greater surprise to you having once said, "God I can't live without this person," that you don't even need to answer the phone.

As much as Summer Ray would rant, she was not going to be able to detach herself from her beloved Gettysburg. Though some accused Summer Ray of chasing after rainbows and dreams and not reality, Summer Ray chose to believe what God had said. She would rather be a fool and get her miracle, than be like the sensible, not taking any risks and ending up with nothing and in misery.

With that decision behind her, and her future in front of her, once home from the skating rink Summer was thankful Kat left her a home cooked meal with a note attached that read, "Thought you could use some cheering up and *remember* I love you!"

Beside the plate of Summer's favorite meal, meatloaf and mashed potatoes was a book Summer had written a few years back titled: " *Your Place In History.*" The book was opened to page 156 that read:

"Love, real love when you find it, don't let it go and don't be afraid of it. Don't allow history to distort it either. History is for the purpose of preservation. But even it can be used in the wrong way. When you hang on to what you need to let go of, when you cannot forgive or forget, when you carry into your future what you lived in the

past, you are allowing history to destroy the happiness you could obtain in your present and future.

If it were not for war, America would not be who she is today. War though hell, defines who men and women are and where they will find their place in history. Let those in future generations who are looking back on you as history, find that your heart was pure before God and let them find that you were the happiest man or woman on earth. Let them find your history full of adventure not bitterness, full of risks and not sidelines, full of goodwill toward men and not evil, and full of the ability try again and not a closed and hardened heart. So much can be accomplished if you just try. Don't deny the love you should be giving and receiving. It isn't just you who loses!"

The words "full of the ability to try again and not a closed and hardened heart" were highlighted in yellow.

Kat knew her friend all too well. She knew that Summer was not a quitter. Summer just needed to be reminded.

Summer said out loud, "Damn you Kathryn Black!"

She knew her friend was right. Summer Ray Sherwood was not a quitter. She was "*more than a conqueror in Christ.*"[j] This war was for her faith. But Summer knew there was so much more to it than that. Her job in Gettysburg was not finished and she knew she had to go back. Come hell or high water, Summer Ray was going to finish her mission. What that mission entailed or would be about, she had no idea. Summer trusted in her God enough to know that He would see to it that she had exactly what she needed to complete whatever assignment He gave her.

CHAPTER TWENTY

Sach's Covered Bridge

"Many waters cannot quench love, neither can the floods drown it."

It is a scripture verse in Song of Solomon verse 8:7. It was part of the poem God had Summer write the other morning. As Summer prayed about what He wanted her to do, the *SPIRIT* told her to drive to "Sach's Covered Bridge."

"Sach's Covered Bridge?" Summer asked. She never heard of it until a tour guide from Billy's field trip had mentioned something about it. Oftentimes when God was trying to get a point across to Summer, He would give her visual understanding. With her brain injury, God knew there were times when Summer just needed extra help. This was one of those times.

Summer told her friend, "No Kat. I don't need you to go with me. But thanks. I have to do this one alone. I will text you when I get there. I love you and thanks for everything. You're the best."

As Summer hung up the phone, she really did not know what the *SPIRIT* was leading her to Sach's Covered Bridge for, she just knew it was where she had to go. The original Sach's Covered Bridge was constructed in the 1850's over Marsh Creek in Adams County. Due to a flood in the 1990's, the bridge was washed out and carried 100 yards downstream. With assistance from the community, the bridge was rescued and restored back to its previous location.

During the Battle of Gettysburg, many wounded and dying soldiers both Union and Confederate, laid upon the banks of the creek, left to rot in the hot summer sun. The brave soldiers' who could actually inch their way down to the creek, perhaps trying to drink the comfort of the cool fresh water, were met with an even more grisly repulsion as the water was red from blood. It had been contaminated from body parts and bodily fluids from other dead soldiers and horses. The sight was so horrid, it made one wonder, how anyone could have survived witnessing such a grotesque display of the cruelty of war, after not dying in combat.

During the aftermath and torrential downpours, imagine rising creek waters, the current of flash floods, drowning the life out of an already vanquishing soldier. As their swollen, butchered bodies floated downstream, is it any wonder that Gettysburg had poltergeists and spirits of the dead aimlessly wandering the town? Why then marvel at the sound of distant cries of agony, or at the sight of vaporous dense fog hovering over the battlefield? Why find it strange that the temperature unexpectedly drops 10 to 20 degrees, or the smell of pipe tobacco suddenly appears when no one is smoking? Though some refuse to believe in apparitions, it had become quite evident to Summer Ray Sherwood that ghosts and spirits most definitely, without a doubt, existed.

A Brand-New Day

When Summer arrived at the bridge, it was a beautiful July morning. The creek was crystal clear, and the refection of the bridge in the water was breathtaking. Looking at the bridge standing tall and majestic, one would never have guessed that it had ever once washed away unless they knew the story before they saw it. The banks, which were full of green grass and shimmering from the sunrays, made it hard to visualize the foul putrid stench of death that had once arrayed it over 147 years prior. As Summer crossed the bridge to the other side, she read the plaque and saw a picture of the original bridge that had been washed out by the flood.

"So, God, You are showing me something about a flood?" She asked as she looked up to Heaven. Summer began to hear the SPIRIT speak softly inside her.

"*When the enemy shall come in like a flood, the SPIRIT of the Lord shall lift up a standard against him,*" was the first thing Summer heard. It was a scripture in Isaiah 59:19. The SPIRIT continued,

> "A flood does not just come from one rain storm or two or even three. A flood comes from torrential rains day after day. Floods are

destructive. They have killed human beings who were caught up in them both physically and emotionally. The force of the water becomes too much for some to bear. Some drown in a sea of sorrow while others drown from nature. Satan knows your weakness. It is there he hits you the hardest by sending one storm after another. But did I not tell you in My Word, " *When you pass through the waters, I will be with you. And through the rivers they shall not overflow you.*"[k] I, my child, have not failed you nor have I forsaken you.

This bridge, though removed from its original site, was brought back and restored. It was made stronger to withstand any more floods that come its way. This is what I am doing with you. I am giving you the desires of your heart and this time it will not be washed away."

Summer began to cry. She knew, had she renounced her faith, she would not have been standing there witnessing a miracle. With the sun shining warm upon her face, she suddenly remembered some of the words to her own poem "*Just Hold On*" she had written in her book the "*The Blessings of Liberty.*"[6]

Though times appear to thunder loud,
And the tides are raging strong.
My dear friend who ever you are,
You've got to just hold on.

I find myself at a loss for words,
When words are what I do.
Look up to Heaven reach for the One,
Who is always there for you.

Please don't let go, or give up the faith,
Though it appears to be black as night.
God loves you, more than you know,
Please don't give up the fight.

A second longer, the sun will shine,
Warm upon your face.

And you will see, eventually,
That you are in a better place.

And all this struggle, heartache and sorrow,
You've held onto so long.
Won't be in today or tomorrow,
Because life has made you strong.

You'll sing with the birds and laugh with the sun,
As new life has come your way.
You'll get passed the darkness of the hour,
To the light of a brand-new day!

Sitting on his horse, Buttercup, the General didn't dare disturb the serene moment that Summer was sharing with her God. The last time he saw her, as she drove out of Gettysburg, she was crying tears of despair. He was happy to finally see tears of joy streaming down her face. Her happiness mattered to him. The realization that Summer's happiness mattered to the General, quite possibly could have been his turning point. Every war has a turning point. The war he fought within himself was finally starting to turn in favor of the real Michael Moses McDaniels.

As he slowly turned his horse to trot off, Summer could see the wind had begun to shift, as a gentle breeze of cold air gusted around her. Though she couldn't see him, Summer Ray knew the General was there. Summer looked up toward Heaven and thanked God for what He was doing. There was much ahead of her, but for now, Summer would just enjoy basking in the love from the God she adored – the God she knew she would never not bow to. Her faith had been tested, her life had been solidified and she was finally on her road to real recovery.

As the Angels that were encamped about her were rejoicing and praising God, back at Devil's Den those slithering, putrid, foul, demonic lowlifes were none too happy. The party they threw in Summer Ray's honor, celebrating her downfall, had unexpectedly and surprisingly been crashed!

Summer Ray Sherwood was back, and the Underworld undoubtedly knew it.

To be continued......

NOTE FROM THE AUTHOR

I am woman who ultimately fears God and who absolutely believes there is a Hell waiting for anyone who does not believe in, nor accepts, the Lord Jesus Christ as their own personal Lord and Savior. I have never been one to cram God down anyone's throat, nor am I one to preach, "hail, fire and brimstone." I believe in doing so, does more harm than good. I am by no means a religious woman. I am simply a woman who loves God and believes in Heaven and in Hell. I have never been one to beg for anything in my life. But, I am so convinced there is a Hell that I am begging you, if you are not yet saved to read a book titled: "*A Divine Revelation of Hell.*" It is authored by Mary K. Baxter. You can find it at most bookstores or online! This is probably the scariest book I have ever read. I wish I could buy it for every human being alive on the planet today! But, since I cannot, I can only refer it.

Although I am an author, publisher and film-maker, I am a Christian first. It is my prayer, by writing this series, that the truth of good vs. evil will ultimately be portrayed in such a way that it will become real to you, the reader, and you, too, will make the decision to make Jesus Christ the Lord of your life! I added the following in case you are ready to make such a decision:

"For God so loved the world that He gave His only begotten Son, that whoever believes in Him should not perish but have everlasting life." John 3:16

"If you confess with your mouth the Lord Jesus Christ and believe in your heart that God raised Him from the dead, you will be saved. For with the heart one believes unto righteousness, and with the mouth confession is made unto salvation. Whoever calls on the name of the Lord shall be saved." Romans 10:9 – 10-13.

Father, in the name of Jesus Christ I come to You. I am a sinner Lord and have sinned against You and against Heaven. I ask you Lord Jesus to forgive my sin and to come into my heart and save my soul. I ask that I be born again into the family of the Living God, and so escape the fires and the torments of eternity in Hell.

I give my life to You. I ask that You will help me to serve You from this moment on. I thank You for saving me and for redeeming me by Your precious Blood. Amen!

My book titled: *"The Blessings of Liberty & 25 Devotions on Freedom, Liberty & Justice...God's Way,"* will also assist you in your walk with the Lord. The following is an excerpt from the back cover.

- Biblically sound – promoting the truth of God's Word
- Historically sound – Revolutionary & Civil Wars, Civil Rights Movement
- Gives insight to the darkest hours of the wars and how our Forefathers persevered through their belief in God

- How our choices today affect our lives tomorrow

- How some of our founding documents are used out of context, therefore promoting demoralization, debauchery and death

- Showing the REAL love of God to those who are ensnared by the devil

- Promotes a positive self-image in knowing who you are in Christ

- Gives understanding and insight to the demonic influence surrounding oppression, depression and possession

Contact and order information – front of the book

REFERENCES

1. At Gettysburg, or What a Girl Saw and Heard of the Battle
   Tillie Pierce Alleman

2. *House of Abraham*
   Lincoln & The Todds – A Family Divided By War
   Stephen Berry
   Publisher: Mariner Books

3. Thomas Paine
   The Quotable Founding Fathers
   Edited by Buckner F. Melton Jr.
   Publisher: Potomac Books

4. *Martine's Handbook of Etiquette*
   Author: Arthur Martine
   Publisher: Applewood Books
   Bedford, Massachusetts

5.   *Nothing Like It In The World*
       Stephen E. Ambrose
       Publisher: Simon & Schuster

6.   *The Blessings of Liberty*
       Author: Juliana Love
       Publisher: Round Top Publishers
       Gettysburg, Pennsylvania

7.   *The Victorian and Civil War Era Weddings*
       Publisher: Pipestone Civil War Days
Committee

8.   *The Enabler*
       Avelyn Miller
       Publisher: Wheatmark Inc.

9.   *Alcoholics Anonymous*

10.   General Robert E. Lee

http://users.bergen.org/ricpan/lee/leesummary.org

11. *They Met AT Gettysburg*
General Edward Stackpole
Publisher Stackpole Books

12. *There Was A Time; A Civil War Romance*
Author: Kenneth Neff Hammontree
Publisher: Living History Productions
Ashland, Ohio 44805

13. *The Present Darkness*
Author: Frank Peritti

14. General George Washington
Treasury of Presidential Quotes
William J. Federer

15. Abraham Lincoln
Abe Lincoln Research Site
RJ Norton

405

16.   President Theodore Roosevelt
       Americanpresidency.org

17.   George Washington
       The Quotable Founding Fathers
       Publisher: Potomac Books

SCRIPTURE VERSES

(a)	Job 38:7
(b)	2 Corinthians 6:18
(c)	Leviticus 17:11
(d)	Genesis 4:10
(e)	Genesis 2:23
(f)	1 John 4:4
(g)	Romans 8:28
(h)	Ephesians 5:11
(i)	Mark 10:9
(j)	Romans 8:37
(k)	Isaiah 43:2
(l)	John 6:53
(m)	2 Corinthians 4:4
(n)	2 Corinthians 4:4

OTHER BOOKS BY AUTHOR

SUMMER RAY SERIES

Volume 2 - Savannah's Calling

Volume 3 - Her Yankee Heart

Volume 4 - The Journey Home

Volume 5 - Time...Begins Again

Volume 6 - The Other Side of Time

Volume 7 - Their Higher Ground

Summer Ray No Matter What!

The Power of Purpose

I Defied...Suicide

The Process of Empowerment

They Laughed At Noah...Till It Rained

The Blessings of Liberty

Detox...The Deceit, Damage, Devil and Doom

Liberal A/MER/I/CA

God's Government vs. Satan's Socialism

Christian's Wake Up!

150th Battle of Gettysburg; Special Photography Edition

The Basic Survival Guide to Beginner Ice Skating

ALL BOOKS CAN BE BOUGHT VIA

AMAZON.COM

THIS FAIR AND BLIGHTED LAND MOVIE
INFORMATION CAN BE FOUND ON OUR
WEBSITE

www.thememoirsofsummerray.com

412

THANK YOU FOR YOUR CONTINUED
SUPPORT OF SUMMER RAY!

WE GREATLY APPRECIATE YOU!

TO KEEP UP WITH THE UPCOMING DIGITAL
MINI-SERIES, PLEASE JOIN OUR MAILING
LIST:

www.julianalove.com

www.thememoirsofsummerray.com

415

40073267R00235

Made in the USA
Middletown, DE
26 March 2019